The Kismet Blade

Terry James Easley

DEDICATION

Thanks to Marsha for putting up with my obsessions.
Also, my gratitude to Bonnie Hearn Hill for teaching me the
craft of storytelling, and that publishing is a tough business.

CONTENTS

ACKNOWLEDGMENTS

Thanks Mom and Dad. Just wish you were still here to enjoy more of the bounty of your labor.

Chapter 1

Ghost Cay

What is that sound? Half awake, Django turned on the air mattress to face the direction of the mystery noise. Ptew. Again. He jackknifed upright. Someone was shooting through the walls of Ghost's tin shack. He quickly scanned the room for Ghost's rifle, couldn't find it, and then jumped into the cast iron bathtub. More bullets cracked through the open door and ricocheted off the hard metal encasement. When the barrage stopped for a second, he peeked over the curled lip of the tub.

"You sons-a-bitches!" Ghost's footsteps clacked against the rickety dock as he ran toward the shanty, dreadlocks bouncing, black shiny legs pumping. Rain, his golden Lab Retriever, barked at his heels. Ghost sprinted through the open door, slammed it shut, grabbed the M16 from under his bed, banged in a clip, and then ripped off a half-dozen rounds toward the speed boat now skimming by his shoreline. "Who the hell did you piss off this time?"

"I dunno, could be anybody." Django said. "Might be Interpol, might be the Raptor's gang." Another errant round whizzed through the air. "Might be just to scare you."

Ghost fired another volley through the open window. "I've seen about everything and I don't scare that easy." He lowered the rifle. "Out of range." He let out a breath that sounded like it came from his toes. Django knew he could hold his breath longer than any man alive. "Now, what's the Raptor?"

"Dude that lives east of Tobacco Cay. Rich mofo."

Ghost peered through his field glasses. "Pretty sure they're gone, for now anyway."

"How do you know they're gone?" Django was in no hurry to emerge from his bathtub fortress.

"Well first of all, Sam's barking would tell us if anything was near the island, and second, you know I'm plugged into these things." Ghost said.

Django unfolded his long frame out of the tub and rubbed Rain's neck. "When did they start shooting at you?"

"Soon as I rounded the corner of the island in my boat. They were waiting. Now, who is this Raptor guy and why's he trying to kill you?"

The Caribbean swelter had drenched Django's shorts and t-shirt. He pulled his shoulder-length hair into a ponytail, and scratched his neck under his beard. The gun battle didn't help his mood much either. "I met the guy online on a website I frequent."

"Is he another grave robber like you?"

Django shook off a cold chill. "You know I don't rob graves. Dealing in art and antiquities is a whole other thing."

Ghost leaned the rifle against the doorframe, and then gathered some driftwood in a pile near the door that looked more like a walk-in freezer door than the found wood door of a traditional Caribbean fishing shack. "Uh huh. So what does he want from you?"

"The Spear of Destiny or Spear of Longinus – the one that pierced the side of Christ at the crucifixion." Django said.

Ghost snickered. "Right. Like you got that spear."

"I do."

"I don't believe it. Show me."

Django reached into his backpack and removed a wooden box about eighteen inches long by two inches wide, and maybe two and a half inches deep, then he carefully opened the ornately carved box to reveal a cracked leather case. Inside the case rested the head of an ancient hammered iron spear, sheathed in gold, wrapped in silver and gold thread, with a prehistoric-looking old nail in the center, circled by another silver band emblazoned with an inscription in Latin that read: "Lancea et clavus Domini".

"What does the Latin say?" asked Ghost.

"Nail of our Lord," said Django. "Nail of the true cross."

"Really - well, it sure looks authentic," Ghost said. "Did you steal it from some museum?"

Django laughed. "From the Schatzkammer Museum in Vienna? Of course not. Even I would have trouble breaking into the Hapsburg Palace. The one on display there isn't the real deal anyway. That one's a fake. This here's the real McCoy." Django held the spear in the air. The afternoon sun filtered through the thatched roof giving the spear a radiant golden specter.

Ghost had started a fire and began cleaning the catch of the day. "How do you know you got the real one? Doesn't everybody say that?"

"Yeah they do, and what with the billions of dollars in counterfeit artifacts floating around, it's a serious challenge to authenticate anything. But I do have an edge - carbon dating, my Garifuna friend." He pointed to the scientific instruments lying next to his backpack. "You might remember that my uncle won the Nobel Prize in Science in 1960 for perfecting carbon-14 dating. I learned a few things from him before he moved on."

Django placed the spear on the driftwood table. Rain

sniffed at it.

"Get away." Ghost waved a conch shell at Rain.

The small beach was littered with these shells, considered a Belizean delicacy. Ghost could have sold the colorful shells on the mainland, in Dangriga, but chose instead to use them to build a sea wall to protect the constantly shifting white sand in front of his shanty. Beyond needing a few dollars for gas and other essentials, money was low on Ghost's priority list.

"Ok, so you stole this from someone else, and supposing it is real, what's the deal between this Raptor cat and the spear?" Ghost asked.

"First of all, I didn't steal it, I traded my whole collection of Amazon artifacts for it. Anyway, the Raptor offered to buy it. He has more money than God. In fact, his goofy followers think he is God, or the Avatar of the age or whatever you want to call him. Some Christians think he's the Anti-Christ. Rumor online is that this is the one piece he needs to complete his mystical artifact collection and come out to the rest of the world as some kind of savior of mankind. He already owns the world. I don't get it."

Ghost chucked a morsel of conch at Rain, who happily slurped it down. The smell of garlic and butter coated the small room. "And you're going to let this guy have it? If my history serves me well, didn't Hitler also have something to do with this piece?"

"Big time," Django said. "Hitler invaded Austria to get it, and then lost it to Patton's forces when the Americans entered Berlin near the close of the War in Europe. The story goes that after American forces secured the spear and some other relics, Hitler put a bullet through his skull less than two hours later. All sorts of world conquerors possessed it, but I have it now."

"Get rid of it," Ghost said. "You gotta protect your own soul, little brother. You white people are all alike. You believe in myth and legend only so far as it lines your pockets."

Django carefully placed the wooden box housing the spear back into his pack. "Maybe, maybe not. But I'm gonna be one rich, white, myth-breaking SOB." Ghost was not in the room. *Where'd he go?* His attention drifted skyward.

Ghost bit off a hunk of conch as he scanned the horizon with his binoculars from the crow's nest above the room. "Maybe," he said. "If fate doesn't rip your balls off first."

Chapter 2

Contact

With his 24-foot sloop tied to Ghost's pier, Django sat on the edge of the gunnel, his bare feet dangling above the diamond-dappled Caribbean. While flat-picking a 12-bar blues riff on his old Harmony guitar, he gazed out, transfixed on a set of foamy waves breaking over the reef.

Rain sat with him, his tongue lapping at the humid air in time with the distant crash of whitewater against coral. The surreal turquoise Caribbean painted a bright impressionist image against the dark canvass of his tortured mind, giving him a borderline migraine.

How was he supposed to get in touch with the Raptor and make the money exchange for the spear? He couldn't just sail over (even if he knew how to get there) and say, "Hi, give me ten million." And then split. Or could he?

In the original plan, The Raptor had told him to leave all traces behind, drop any vestiges of his former life, rent a sailboat in Miami under a fake name, and then sail to the one of the small islands near Tobacco Cay. From that point, when the Raptor had verified Django's compliance, a meeting would be arranged. *I've done all that, now what?*

The pace was wearing him down. He'd been on the run from pursuers for the last two months, although he didn't know exactly who they were, but he could feel their presence at every traffic light, every ticket kiosk, every watering hole. It was like that spooky feeling he always got after he turned off the lights in the house in Berkeley and walked toward the bedroom and Celeste. Unseen eyes were always nearby, always watching him in the dark.

Maybe they were Germans, who believed they were the rightful owners of the Spear, maybe Austrians, maybe artifact pirates who may or may not be agents of the Raptor. Yet, any way he cut it, whoever had shot up Ghost's shack, didn't care whether he lived or died, as long as they got the Spear of Destiny.

"Little meditation?" Ghost's voice ripped through his head. Two Beliken beers dangled from one of his hands, the M16 was cradled in the other.

"Don't do that, man." Django reached for a beer. "You got any pain reliever I can wash down with this skunk piss?"

"You got the only pain reliever I ever use." Ghost took a swig of Belize's best brew. "You can't stay here, you know that, right? As much as I care about you, I can't have a war going on. Messes up my fishin'."

Django nodded. He knew that the sea and fishing was everything to Ghost, keeping him away from his family in Dangriga for days on end. They first met more than twenty-five years ago when Django was a teenager on a solo sailing trip around the world. He had run into a squall off Cuba, as had Ghost, who'd been fishing off its eastern coast, near the southwestern end of the Bermuda Triangle. A violent norther forced them both to seek refuge in the waters off Cojimar - the bay where Ernest Hemingway had kept his fishing boat. Over a few beers while they waited out the passing of the storm, Ghost and Django discovered that, besides solo navigation, they shared a love for The Old Man and the Sea, esoteric literature, and treasure - spiritual and otherwise.

Back on the dock, Rain started to pace and whine. Ghost sipped his beer as he peered out at the waves. "Rough night, man?"

"Yeah, I'm kinda screwed, you know. My cell phone drowned in the sail over, and I have no way of reaching the Raptor, or Celeste for that matter."

"Celeste? Hmm."

"You remember Celeste? We've been together…well, sort of together ever since our undergraduate days at

Berkeley."

"Oh yeah, I know all about it." Ghost stared hard at the horizon, then put his finger on the trigger of the rifle. "You see that?"

The same black cigar boat from yesterday appeared out of the mist that hung over the rippled sparkling surface.

"Looks like they might be cruising out by the reef." His voice was low.

"I see them." Django grabbed his field glasses from the starboard locker. "Assholes. Who are those guys?"

Ghost was focused on the black boat. "That spear of yours makes you the most powerful man in the world, right? Why don't you just make 'em disappear?"

Django moaned. "Oh, man, I don't believe in fairytales." He grabbed his .45 caliber Smith and Wesson from the starboard boat locker, checked the clip on the semi-automatic, and then shoved it in the back waistband of his cut-off Levi's. The cool black steel against his sweaty backside reminded him that the SW99 would stop any man or shark – if the target got within range. Or blow his own ass off. "People make their own voodoo icons to justify their dreams and behavior," he said. "What would I do with power? I want the dinero."

"You may want to reconsider before it's too late, bud." Ghost shouldered the rifle, put his hand on the railing, and swung aboard the vessel. "All you really leave this earth with is your eternal soul."

"Yeah, yeah, I know, I know." Django put up his hand like a stop sign. "But, while I'm spinning on this E ticket ride, I'm a grabbin' for the brass ring."

Rain barked. In unison, they jerked around to the unmistakable roar of the cigar boat's Mercedes-Benz racing engine, and then, just as quickly, they dove behind the protection of the gunnel wall. Ghost clicked off his safety. Django did the same on the pistol. They both had their sights trained on the black dot. When the craft got within shooting distance of the M16, it abruptly swerved southward and then disappeared again into the vapor.

Django let out a gasp of air. "Whew, I need another beer." He opened one from the stash in his cooler and gave one to Ghost. "You know, the more I think about it, those aren't the Raptor's people." He wiped the cold bottle across his forehead. "All of his boats and planes are marked with the solar cross."

"Which one?" Ghost asked.

"A black circle with a red kind of Maltese cross in the middle – The Knight's Templar insignia. Besides, he needs me for the spear. I gotta reach this dude - but my phone is junk."

Ghost smiled. "Look up there." He pointed to a dish at

the top of the palm tree closest to his tin shack.

"Satellite?"

"All the comforts of home." The gold in his teeth sparkled in the sun.

"Well, shit," Django said. "You didn't tell me you were connected. You got a computer?"

"Puter and satellite phone."

"Well, let's get after it." He jumped to his feet. "Where is it?"

"Hidden under the bed, where I keep the rifle." Ghost climbed up on the dock. "You were sleeping right next to it."

Django was already jogging toward the shack. Rain bounced ahead of him, his tail slashing the thickening morning dew. "Is it a PC or a MAC? What's the password?" He never turned to get an answer.

"Tell him to scoot on over in his rocket ship and pick you up," Ghost yelled.

In the shack, Django fumbled with the laptop. He could never get these damned things opened in a hurry. "I'm going to tell him to come and get me."

"You can't do that." With the red bandana that had been tied around his neck, Ghost wiped his sweat away. "I don't want him to know about this place."

"Relax man, he probably knows anyway. Besides, he

doesn't want anything you have. I've got the spear. It's me he wants."

"What makes you think he won't just eliminate you and grab the spear?"

"Because I won't have it. I'm going to leave it here with you."

"Oh, right." Ghost shook his head. "Perfect idea."

Django searched the familiar antiquities website, and squinted at the words. "I think he's online now." He searched Ghost's face. "Are you going to help me, or what?"

"I'll tell you what I'll do." He rubbed his square jaw, then tapped his index finger against the dimple in his chin. "I don't like this idea I'm about to offer. We'll take the satellite phone – it's got GPS built in – we'll take it out on the boat and then we can give the Raptor the coordinates where we are, and he can come and get you. Don't forget to get his number. I'll take you out beyond Tobacco Cay and fish while we wait for him."

Django grinned, then turned and typed furiously. "He says he's got a helicopter with floats, and agrees to pick me up." Rain licked his hands as they flew over the keyboard. Finally, he stopped typing and stared out toward the open sea.

Ghost stood in the open doorway and threw last night's

dinner conch shell outside. When it landed, it clacked like a cue ball colliding with the rest of the rack, until it came to rest among the other thousands of rainbow-colored calcium crystal shells comprising the sea wall. "You know, if this cat's as cool as you make him out to be, he probably, unfortunately, already has a lock on you."

Django was in no mood for negativity. "Okay, It's a done deal, let's roll." His pulse raced. The blood was returning to his head.

"And what about Celeste?" Ghost asked. "We both owe her an explanation."

"What? We?" Django was startled. "Let me have the sat phone. I'm calling her right now."

Chapter 3

Celeste Norris

Celeste Norris fumbled with the key to her front door. She heard the last ring of her telephone before the answering machine clicked on. By the time she finally stumbled through the stacks of books and easels with unfinished paintings, the message was done. She pushed the button to rewind and then retraced her steps to retrieve the scattered papers left in her wake.

"Hey babe, it's you're one and only here." *Django you friggin turd.* "Sorry, I won't get home this week. I had some urgent business in Belize. I can't tell you everything right now, but I promise to get back to you when I knock this thing out. It's gonna be good for both of us. Keep the light on. Love you." Click.

She threw the beige pillow as hard as she could at the couch. Pancho, her cat, hissed like a snake and flew into the bedroom. The stay-at-home sabbatical was a welcomed vacation from teaching her art classes at Cal, but she wanted to spend the time with Django, and he'd promised to get back to Berkeley when her break started. This was one toke over the line.

There was a knock at the front door. Through the lower frames of the beveled glass the familiar wrinkled face with too much make-up bobbed through the prism panes. In the afternoon golden glow, Jane Cook, her next-door neighbor, with that shock of white hair, flickered like a circus clown in a Fellini movie.

It would have been funny if she weren't in such a hurry. She had to reposition the partially unrolled Dutch Master that had blown across the path of the door.

"Hello, dear." Jane protected a large painting that rested against her frail body. She was having some difficulty with the obviously heavy, mounted canvass that stretched from the wooden porch nearly to her armpits. "I hate to bother you, but that nice gentleman in the brown truck came again today and left a package. You know how I hate to be nosey, but I took the liberty to open it for you."

"That's sweet of you. Won't you come in? Sorry, the place is a mess." As if it ever looked any different. "Can I fix you a cup of tea?"

"Kind of you to offer." Jane never turned down

anything. "It looks like another one of your paintings."

Celeste quickly took it from her and wedged it in the corner with the rest of the artwork. "Thank you for being so attentive. If you'll excuse me, while the water is heating, I have to pack a bag."

Jane ambled toward the kitchen. She always seemed fascinated by the boiling process. "Are you going somewhere, dear?"

"Yes, I have to make a quick business trip to Belize. I hate to impose, but could you take care of Pancho and watch the place for me for a week or so?"

"Of course I will. I have nothing else to do except watch my shows." Jane wandered into the bedroom. "You're not chasing that old scoundrel Django again, are you?"

"I might see him while I'm down there." She sat at her art deco vanity, and then took her passport out of the top drawer. In the reflection in the mirror, the afternoon sun painted sepia streaks across the bedroom. Everything they owned together in this Victorian house was old: the furniture, dishes from garage sales, vinyl albums stacked in milk crates, charcoal drawings intertwined with his masks from South America, her copies of Renaissance paintings, his shrunken heads from Africa, a hash pipe from Viet Nam.

"It's none of my business," Jane said. "But, I wish

you'd find someone else who would treat you like you deserve. Like one of those nice professors you teach with."

"You're right, Jane. It's none of your business."

"I'm sorry, dear, it's just that I worry about your future. You're still young. Well, 40s is young to me. And pretty. I remember when I had long brown curly hair too. And it's just that I think you should settle down and raise a family."

Oh shit, that familiar refrain. She looked at the crow's feet starting to form around the corners of her blue eyes. *Maybe Jane was right.*

Never one to dither when she was on a mission, she'd packed her clothes and was ready to boogie. "Could you drive me to the Oakland airport?"

Jane hesitated and played with her dangling earring. "Uh, of course I will. You know I don't drive that much anymore, and I'm not positive the old Buick will start and I'm not sure how to get there, and - "

Celeste clutched her arm. Together they swept into the parlor where she grabbed the Garmin from the top of a stack of essays. "You can use this GPS. I have my IPhone anyway. I showed you how to use this, remember?"

"I forgot."

"The airport address is saved on the screen you're looking at. All you have to do is press this thingy when you get in the car, and this button that says 'home' when you're ready to leave the airport." She waved her hand in the air like a Vegas magician. "And voila, you're home, ET."

"Uh, uh, I don't know dear, this stuff kinda rattles me a little. "

By now, with Jane in tow, Celeste had the key in the lock. She whisked up Pancho and kissed him on the nose.

"It's no problem, believe me. If you get lost, stop any cop on the street or any student for that matter. You also know my cell. Friendly town, remember. Here's the key. Me casa, su casa, and so forth." She snatched her leather jacket and Panama hat from the hall tree rack, and then locked the door behind them.

"What about the tea?"

She must be losing it. She ran back into the house and turned off the gas.

Back outside, Jane looked like one of those ghosts she always talked about. "Will I hear from you? Should I worry? What if there's an emergency?"

"D, all of the above. You have a support system, darlin', right in your hand." Celeste couldn't move fast enough. "Now, let's rock and roll, granny."

Chapter 4

The Raptor

The conversation with Django completed, the Raptor
pushed away from his desk to survey the two-story wall of
video screens that surrounded him. While he savored the
sensation of being in charge of his domain, he was sorry he
had created the online avatar that had become his evil
identity to some of his detractors. He preferred his given
name Mohammed or Mr. Goldman. Some used the term
Master, but that wasn't quite right. Not yet anyway.

He rotated his desk chair three hundred and sixty
degrees so that he could monitor his empire and the various
departments of the island complex. From his command
center he could monitor any channel around the world or
spy on anyone with his own satellite network. *That poor
fool Django.*

A light in front of him flashed. He pushed the
corresponding button to fill the wall across from his desk

with the one image. "Everything on target. Forty-eight hours to East Jerusalem." *Perfect.*

He loved the fact that his command center stayed a comfortable sixty-eight degrees a thousand feet below the surface of the island. It had taken over thirty-five years to get to the point of total dominion and sovereignty, but it had been worth it. He stared at the picture of his father Sheik Mohammed Al Maktoum. *We will prevail.*

His daughter, Lydia, entered his chambers. "The choppers are ready, sir."

In the twenty-five years since he'd stolen the infant away from a Palestinian family in occupied Gaza, he still marveled at her doll-like beauty, athletic body, piercing ebony eyes, long shoulder-length black hair that outlined her face, reminding him of onyx and topaz. She had the brains and physical dexterity to match. So what if people said he looked like the late Aristotle Onassis, he had her face to front the empire.

"I want you to go to Ghost's shack and see what you can find." He stood to face her eye to eye. "While I entertain our friend Django." She bowed and left the room.

He knew Lydia would do anything for him. Together they had been monitoring Django since he left Miami.

He picked up the three books he'd been perusing, and walked down the hallway to place them back on the bookshelf with the rest of his current research texts. As he gazed down the row of a collection that disappeared into the vanishing point, he felt proud that his vast library of esoteric literature rivaled any in the world. He slid the Torah, the Quran and the King James Bible into their gold-outlined receptacles.

His mastery of the major disciplines of the world had been a lifelong quest. After his oil-rich father had made sure he was born in Bethlehem and received his early religious training in Saudi Arabia and Lebanon, he'd sent his young son to the United States to study with the Jesuits, so that he would be well steeped in secular and comparative religious knowledge, and the power of the order.

His Chief of Staff, Nadar, entered the book depository. Tall, turbaned and imposing, he shadowed the light spilling into the underground corridor. "Sir, you might find an interesting development on Al Jazeera television."

Nadar preceded him into the communications room. "It appears that the Eastern Coalition troops are rapidly gathering in the Iranian Theater."

He sat at his desk and clicked on the switches marked Al Jazeera, CNN, and the BBC. Three screens jumped to life in front of him.

"Right on schedule."

Nadar moved to the front of the desk. "Sir, I have a

half-dozen international networks wishing to conduct an interview with you. They all know our policy of no press, but since news of war in the Middle East is escalating, and given the leaked report in *Mother Jones* that you were supplying armaments to both sides, well, I think we need to say something."

"Tell them we are in negotiations at this time and urging all sides toward moderation. That we implore all parties to step back from the brink of war." He sipped from his cranberry sharbat. "That ought to hold them until I give them the news they all long for."

"And then there is the issue of Mr. Django Roth and his relic." Nadar cleared his throat. "What would you like us to do about him? The object has a locator chip imbedded in it, but, we suspect he has altered it. However, we are confident we can find it."

The Raptor played with a small anti-gravity gyroscope that projected DNA type multi-colored spirals across the plasma screens as it spun in midair.

"Tell Django that I'm coming, but send the double. I don't trust him. Then bring him and the object into my chambers. I'll take it from there."

Suddenly, red lights began flashing, and sirens bleated. He punched up Security and Maintenance. Two screens popped to life. "What's going on?"

Maintenance spoke first. The monitor filled with the ashen face of the Superintendent, Denver Green. "We have a reactor cooling malfunction, sir."

"Shut off that irritating alert." He glared at his Chief of Security.

"Is that wise sir?" The Chief asked.

"Don't ask questions. Just get away from my face and do it. Nobody leaves the island." The veins in his neck tightened, as he walked toward the screen. "Do you understand?"

"Yes, sir."

The Security panel went dark. He now had only Denver to deal with. "Okay, give me the bottom line," he said.

"Well, sir." The Superintendent swallowed hard. "We've had a power spike in our auxiliary generator that caused us to lose some coolant in the reactor. That caused the alarm to go off."

"All right." He tossed the gyroscope down the hall where it turned and headed down another corridor-spoke of the command wheel. "What are the outside odds of a release or even a meltdown?"

Denver checked his instruments. "I would say it's very remote, sir, but I think we should exert every precaution and evacuate the island except for essential personnel."

"Nonsense. That's the very last thing I want to do." He

edged closer to the screen. "I don't want you to leave that control room, nor do I want you to breathe a word of this to anyone else. Do you have that, Mr. Green?"

"Yes, sir." The screen collapsed into blackness.

He picked up the house phone and punched up the Assistant to the Chief of Security. "Conrad, did the Chief give you my instructions?" he asked.

"Yes, sir. That there is no emergency." His delivery was clear and steady. "It was a false alarm, and no one can leave the island."

He couldn't see the assistant's face, but having been trained in the art of emotion recognition and manipulation, he knew by the tone in his voice that Conrad would comply. "Did he tell you anything else?"

"No, sir."

"Excellent." He unlocked the top right drawer, pulled a .38 special out and stuck it in his linen jacket pocket. " One other thing," he said. "There has been a change of plans. I want the jet and crew to be able to fly to the Middle East. I will give the final destination in midair. I want to be ready within the hour."

"Consider it done, sir."

Seconds-in-command were sometimes more valuable than the chiefs with whom he often had to share personal information. Besides, Conrad was a career climber with virtually no discernible weakness for ethics. The chain of command was intact.

An hour later, fully packed, from his quarters on the fifth floor, Mohammed walked toward the elevator. His pocket phone buzzed. The text read: "We have Django on the flight deck."

"Keep everyone there until I arrive in a few minutes." He hit the send button, and then punched in a text to Lydia.

"Do you have the prize?" She would know it was the spear. He had to be very careful with classified information at this juncture. Someone could have breached communication security.

"We have it, sir. Where do you want it?"

"Bring it to the flight deck and wait for me there."

He was now on the second level outside the Chief's private quarters. Delicately, he knocked on the door.

"Come on in." When the Chief saw it was his boss, he tried to rise, but Mohammed motioned for him to stay seated.

The Raptor moved to sit on the bed. "What are you working on?"

When the Chief turned to his paperwork on the desk, Mohammed grabbed a pillow, quickly put it near the back of the Chief's head and fired three rounds into the base of his skull, that drove his bloodied head to the desktop. He calmly reloaded and then departed for the flight deck.

Once he was ready to board the already humming Learjet, Lydia delivered the prize in a large paper sack. Then, Django walked up, secure in the grasp of the Raptor's double.

"What the hell?" Like a wind-up toy, Django's head ratcheted back and forth between the two men who were already pushing and pulling him up the boarding steps.

Once in their seats and buckled down, Mohammed watched Django's anger and frustration grow every second. "Settle down and relax my friend," he said. "We have a long ride."

Django craned his neck and peered out of the porthole. "I can't do this. Besides, we have business, plus we don't have the spear. Where you taking me?"

Mohammed jerked the Spear out of the bag and hoisted it with a flourish. Then he smiled. "We now have everything we need. And you, my friend," he said, as he pushed back in his reclining seat. "Will tell me everything I need to know about how to utilize this magical relic on our journey to Tehran."

Chapter 5
Ghost

Ghost felt the familiar chill run across his shoulders, the one that caused him to carry the M16, and see everything like there was a third eye in the back of his head. He didn't feel good about Django's helicopter pick up. Something was wrong. He had to find out what his body was trying to tell him.

He shut down his 50-horse Mercury outboard motor and coasted into the dock. A flash of light near the back of the shack caught his eye. Rain jumped to the pier from ten feet out and sprinted like he spotted running game.

Before he could tie off, the roar of a jet boat pierced the afternoon air. He caught a glimpse of the Templar Cross as the vessel blasted south, out of range in seconds.

The door to the shack lay open. Rain stood at the threshold looking sad. The shanty had been completely ransacked. The few tables and chairs had been tossed against the tin siding leaving dents and holes everywhere. Kitchenware, fishing gear, and bedding were scattered like a Caribbean hurricane had struck. Django's scientific equipment lay in shambles against the back wall. Most importantly, the Spear that had been wrapped and placed under the bed was gone.

He stood the kitchen tables and chairs back in place. He sat and laid his head on the table. Must be what rape felt like. Rain rested his head on his thigh.

The low hum of a different boat engine broke the silence. He sprang to his feet, and then turned off the safety on the M16. Ready to fire, he had the approaching boat in his sights.

"Ghost, don't shoot," a woman shouted, silhouetted against the sparkling water. "It's Celeste. It's me, Celeste."

The commercial island hop ferry cruised into the dock. The deck hand threw the bowline to Ghost. He tied the front of the boat off, and then secured the stern line to the rear cleat. From the starboard railing, Celeste jumped into his arms, nearly knocking him over. Rain barked and danced in a circle.

He pushed back from her clutching embrace. "Man, what a sight for sunburned eyes. I sure didn't expect you this soon. You look like a million bucks."

Celeste's face turned red. "You're so kind. I got here

pretty quick because I had good connections. I lucked out and caught the express out of Belize City."

He grabbed her bag and they walked down the pier. "I gotta tell you, the place doesn't look quite the same since you were here a couple years ago. We got hit."

She stopped in her tracks. "What? Hit? Where's Django? Is he all right?"

"Django's fine." He had to tell a white lie.

They stopped at the door. "Oh, my God," she said. "Who did this?"

"I'm not positive," he said. "But I believe it was the Raptor's gang."

"And who is the Raptor?" she asked.

"Probably the richest, most powerful man in the world. He owns a cay about forty miles from here."

"And he and Django are involved because –"

"Because Django is trying to sell him the Spear of Christ." He picked up a knife from the floor. "This guy has some crazy notion that he can save the world or something if he has the spear."

She looked baffled. "How did Django get to the island?"

"I took him out to a fishing spot, and then a helicopter came and picked him up."

"We have to go to Raptor Island," she said. "He's in

trouble."

"That place is like an army base." Ghost picked up Django's scientific instruments and placed them back in their leather carrying case. "Could be dangerous. Are you up for that?"

"After hangin' with Django for nearly twenty years, I'm ready for anything."

Rain barked and danced.

"You may not be ready for this guy," he replied.

"One thing I don't get," she said. "Why would he leave the spear here when you guys left in the boat?"

"Well, he figured it was a straight business deal, but didn't want to show the real goods too early. Now, I'm not so sure it was the right move to leave him alone with this Raptor dude."

Celeste looked through Django's leather instrument bag. "You know," she said. "The more I think about it, the more I question that he'd leave the spear out in the open. He usually has some kind of backup plan."

Ghost knew him pretty well, too. Sailing together and playing poker on extended trips told you a lot about a man. "He was in a hurry to make this happen. It was his idea to leave it under the bed. But still."

"Hey, there's some kind of electronic device in here," she said.

"You don't suppose?" Ghost handled the silvery object that looked like a television remote control.

"It would be just like him," she said. I've seen this kind of tracking device before. What if he had a duplicate with a chip in it and hid it somewhere around here?"

"Let's find out." He turned the gadget on, and it jumped to life.

"If this is a locator, and the spear has a sending unit in it," she said. "Why wouldn't the Raptor's people also use one?"

"They didn't need to. They found it in plain sight."

"He's a smart cookie," she said. "Where do you want to start?"

The late afternoon sun had heated up the room. He took off his shirt and grabbed the shovel. "Let's start behind the shack."

They moved slowly, watching the digital lights on the locator. Soon the red LEDs flashed, and it started to beep. He located the hottest spot in the sand where the chirps were nearly continuous. A couple of feet away from his lookout palm tree, he began to dig. At eighteen inches, the shovel hit something solid.

He tossed the locator to Celeste, and then dug furiously with his hands until he had a grip on a wooden box. "We got something," he told her.

He laid the box in the sand, and she bent to examine it with him.

"Well," she said. "Open the dang thing."

He clapped his hands together to get rid of the excess sand and then rubbed what was still sticking to his sweaty palms on his shorts. The lid creaked open.

"There she is," he said.

Celeste wiped her forehead with the back of her hand. "Wow."

"Looks just like the other one."

They stared transfixed until Rain barked.

On the horizon, the sun was making its final plunge. The orange glow enveloped both of them.

"Now what?" she asked.

His gaze followed the lengthening shadows of the palms, across the rippling water to the northeastern horizon. "We leave in the morning," he said. "Tonight we sleep."

"I don't think so," she replied.

Chapter 6

The Crossing

Ghost slowed the motor to ease his fishing boat upward through another four-foot swell. Rain perched just below the bow, balanced like a four-footed sentry. Celeste sat on the forward bench near him, facing Ghost.

At least they were fortunate enough to have a nearly full moon on such a choppy night. He had not wanted to take the boat to Raptor Cay with these seas, but Celeste had insisted. He knew she was right. They had to find Django.

"How do I keep from getting seasick," she begged.

"On a larger boat, I'd tell you to stand in the middle, take the swells with your legs and watch a steady point on the horizon." He cut back the throttle again. "But tonight in my boat, it's just mind over matter."

"Gee, thanks," she said.

The satellite phone rang. Now he had the boat, Celeste, and the caller to deal with. He had to take it, so he just stopped the boat. A wave crashed over the bow, tumbling

Rain, and soaking Celeste. She vomited into the foam.

"Shit," she yelled. "Why'd you stop this damn thing?"

"Because the phone is ringing, and it could be Django," he shouted.

She stumbled to the back of the boat. "Give me the phone, and you get this tuna boat crankin'."

"Could be Regina," he said.

"If it's your wife, I'll tell her we're in a hurricane screwing our brains out." She glared. "Now give me the phone."

"Very funny." Reluctantly, he handed it to her as a swell sent her into his lap.

"Hello," she yelled. "Who is this?"

"You'll have to speak up." She coughed. "We're not exactly in an office out here."

The water calmed enough for Ghost to grab the phone. "Who is this?"

"Ghost?" The voice was faint.

"Django, is that you?"

"Yes. Was that Celeste?"

"Yes it was."

"How in the world?" Django's strained voice trailed off. "Never mind, I don't have much time. I'm not on the island. We're headed to Tehran on the Raptor's jet. Did they get the real spear?"

A loud mechanical bang drowned out his voice. He heard the sound of bodies colliding, followed by an animal-like scream, then a crack like a bat hitting a baseball. A sickening groan, then the line went dead.

Ghost fought a chill that crept along his shoulders, and then headed down his spine.

"Oh Lord," he mumbled.

"What?" Celeste stood over him. Her moonlit face reminded him of both witches in the Wizard of Oz at the same time. "What?" she yelled.

"Sit down."

She didn't budge. "Can you see I'm upset?"

"Okay," he said. "Django's not on the island. He's on his way to what sounded like Tehran with the Raptor." He couldn't bring himself to tell her about the dogfight he'd just heard.

She covered her face with both hands. Sobbing, she collapsed like a net onto the slick floor of the boat.

He took off his weather poncho and covered her. "It's going to be okay," he said and stroked her wet hair. "We'll find him."

Ghost looked at his diving watch, and then checked his GPS. The island loomed ahead. Celeste had been asleep for the last three hours, and now it was high time she joined the boarding party. He nudged her. Rain licked her face.

"Yo, sleeping beauty."

She groaned, sat up and gazed at the moon. "Where are we?" she asked.

"About ten minutes from the island." He poured some water from the five-gallon jug onto a rag and handed it to her. "Wipe your face, darlin'. We may have some company."

Cutting the engine to a purr, he glided into a mooring, parallel to the carpeted dock. He quickly jumped out, first tying off the bow to the polished brass cleat, then the stern line.

Once secured, he pulled the box containing the Spear out of his pack and let Rain sniff it. Then, he placed it under his seat next to the gas can. "Stay and keep guard," he said. Rain held his position in the boat, glancing at the spear. Then he barked softly one time.

Ghost helped Celeste up onto the dock. They climbed the ladder to the top of the pier and looked around.

"Man, this is some set-up," he said. "It looks like the deck of an aircraft carrier."

"Except for the coning towers and mountain," she replied. "Sorry I kinda flaked out on you."

"That's okay. The sea stayed calm, and gave me plenty of time to think. Besides, I knew you were totally fried."

She wiped her face again with the damp cloth. "So, what's the plan? Have you got a magic carpet to fly us from here to the Middle East?"

"As if." He managed a thin smile. "I am kind of surprised no one is here to greet us."

"I doubt that they get many visitors, " she said. "Especially in the middle of the night."

In an instant they were bathed in a spotlight that felt like the stage lighting Ghost sweated under when he played drums on the mainland. But no one was clapping. Instead, two armed guards, accompanied by a dark, smaller person, marched quickly toward them.

The guards seized them.

"My name is Lydia." The shorter woman was obviously in charge.

"So you – "

"Stop." She held up her hand. "I know who you are."

Their bodies restrained, Ghost and Celeste could only exchange glances.

"The sentries will escort you to a place where we can chat," she said. "You'll have to forgive our arrangements on such short notice." Then, she turned and left.

The guards led them to a glass elevator in the side of the mountain. As they began their descent into the earth, Ghost pointed toward the runway.

"Is that a Harrier Jump Jet?" he asked.

The guards looked in the direction of the sunrise glow on the horizon, but did not speak. Their brief distraction allowed Ghost to quickly elbow the closest guard in the neck. Immediately, he dropped lifeless to the floor. As the other guard lunged at him, Celeste grabbed him around the neck. As they struggled, Ghost kneed the guard in the groin, and then floored him with an uppercut to the jaw.

Celeste put her head down and tried to catch her breath. "This is nuts," she said.

The last guard to hit the floor moaned. Ghost grabbed his rifle and silenced him with a blow to the back of his head.

He knelt down and began to unbutton the guard's jacket.

"What in the world are you doing?" she asked.

"We're going to put on these uniforms and then try to find out what's going on around here?"

"What good is that going to do?"

"Remember that jet on the tarmac?"

"Well, yeah."

"Somebody around here has to know how to fly it," he told her. "We're not going to get a taxi service to Iran."

"What about the boat?" she asked. "Rain and the spear are still there."

"I'm working on that."

He put on the guard's ceremonial bearskin hat and gave the other one to Celeste.

"Tuck your hair under this thing."

"Yuck," she said. "It feels like it's alive."

He chuckled. "It was at one time."

The elevator stopped on B5. The door opened to what looked like a hotel wing of rooms. As the doors squeezed shut again, they finished putting on the uniforms, then he pushed the open button. He spotted a janitorial sign and motioned for Celeste to help him drag the men into the room.

"This is great," she said. "A couple of clowns in goofy hats dragging half naked men into a cleaning room."

Ghost clamped his hands under the second guard's shoulders.

"Can you please keep it down," he whispered.

A hip-hop song drifted from the speakers in the corridor. The air smelled like curry and fish. Luckily, the hall was empty.

"Now what, El Capitan?" She put her hands on her hips.

"Now we find Lydia," he said. "My gut tells me she's got some answers."

Chapter 7

Flight to Tehran

The plane shook, jarring Django from his semi-coma. His head felt like a split watermelon – the overripe kind like the ones he used to bombard in his mom and dad's patch at the Hog Farm commune. He couldn't help his ailing father much in this predicament.

The endless water far below the cabin of the Learjet reminded him of the pain he caused himself by chasing the carrot of success. How far was he going to have to go to get rich or die in the process? The Raptor's arrogant smile from the seat facing him increased his resolve to beat this lunatic.

Django gritted his teeth. "What the hell did you hit me with?"

The Raptor showed him the butt of the .38 in his pocket. "The equalizer," he said. "You better hope I don't have to use the other end on you."

"So what about the spear?" He wiped the dried blood

off the side of his face with his assailant's cocktail napkin. "I believe you owe me some money and an explanation."

The Raptor stirred his drink and laughed. "Money should be the last thing on your mind. It's time you told me how to invoke the power of the relic or you might find yourself flying out of here to end up as fish food on the bottom of the Atlantic."

How was he supposed to do that? There was no magic, only history. He had to think of something fast.

"I'm the only one who can invoke the power," Django said. "Magic like this doesn't come easy. It takes deep study of the esoteric consequences."

The Raptor stood and grabbed him by the collar. "Bullshit," he yelled. "I am the master of the metaphysical. You will tell me right now or I will have Jason throw you out of the jet."

"That's not much of an offer."

Remaining cool was getting to be a problem. Django wanted to drop this nut job, but his bodyguard – who had to be Jason - had emerged from the flight deck and hovered nearby like a vulture on road kill.

"Now give me the incantation or whatever the code is," the Raptor demanded.

"It's not that easy." His mind raced. "You should know that the spell, like all rituals, is based on paganism. I have to be in contact with the earth to conjure the power."

The Raptor still held his collar and glared down. "If I find you are lying, I will kill you on the spot."

"Now let go of my collar," he said. "So I can meditate and prepare to summon that source."

The Raptor snapped his fingers, and the goon was beside them.

"Jason, I want you to help Mr. Roth get cleaned up, and then I would like you to find a suit for him in the wardrobe closet. I'm sure there will be something in there that will be appropriate for a business meeting."

The attendant bowed and walked to the back of the plane. He found a suit and beckoned for Django to come to the rear, where he stood at the propped-open door to the lavatory.

In front of a mirror for the first time in longer than he could remember, Django stared at his face. Near the top of his left cheekbone, an egg-sized knot raised like a red island surrounded by black and gray speckled hair. Dried blood flecked his beard, making him look like a dazed combat veteran. His eyes were black holes spinning into a brain filled with dark questions.

He washed his face and sponged off the rest of his body, trimmed his beard as best he could, drug a comb through his shoulder-length hair, then found a rubber band,

and pulled it into a ponytail. Half way into brushing his teeth, Jason shoved him a white shirt and tie, along with a black suit.

When he was finished, he stood back to look at himself. "Perfect ensemble," he said. "For a Gothic funeral."

Jason's silence spoke volumes about his sense of humor.

"Sir, we have been cleared to land in Tehran." The pilot's voice was calm as it crackled over the speaker system. "So, may I ask you and your guest to please buckle up. We should be on the ground in about fifteen minutes."

When Django returned to his seat, the Raptor stood as if to greet a gentleman.

"Amazing transformation, Mr. Roth."

Django looked out the window. The blue of the water had turned to sandy desert.

"Are we going to a camel barbecue?" he asked.

"No, we are not," he answered. "As a matter of fact, we will be attending a meeting of some of the world's most influential citizens."

"You mean a gang of terrorists who are preparing to invade Israel, don't you?" He shifted in his seat and tugged at the collar of his shirt. "In my business, it pays to follow the news."

"So, you know about the intrigue in the Middle East?"

Jason brought two glasses of cranberry juice and warm towels.

Django dabbed at his wound. "Who do you guys think you are to threaten the peace of the whole world?"

The Raptor wiped his perspiring face. "You, my friend, are merely a capitalistic mercenary passing through history, while I am the Avatar here to change that history."

"You mean to tell me that you think you are Mohammed, Jesus, Buddha – the Perfect Master returned?"

"I am that I am," he said.

"Holy shit," Django blurted. This was even weirder than he'd imagined.

The landing gear clattered beneath the plane. Below, the city of nearly nine million souls stretched to the base of the snow-covered Alborz Mountains to the north. A brown layer of smog looked more menacing than it had years ago when he had been to Tehran on an artifact hunt.

"When we are on the ground," The Raptor said, "You will be watched by armed guards at all times. We will be escorted directly to the meeting. Because you will have the spear and its harnessed power, you will sit next to me and act as my spiritual advisor."

Django swallowed hard. He'd worn a lot of hats in his life, but this would be his first gig as a shaman.

"You might tell me how I am supposed to advise you,"

he replied.

The Raptor smiled. "You will psychically support my aura of invincibility. With the Spear of Christ, nothing can stop me."

"So let me get this straight, the spear is your Philosopher's Stone that will alchemically transmute you into becoming the Messiah?" Django couldn't believe his own words. "Is that actually what you are saying?"

"I couldn't have stated it better myself."

The wheels screeched as the racing jet bounced on the tarmac. It felt like this missile he was strapped to would never get stopped at the end of the runway. He had to get a grip. Lord have mercy, he'd seen crazy, but how was he going to dodge this one? Of course, he always had the spear to fall back on.

He almost laughed. What a crazy image that was. Although the lance was still a dangerous weapon, it was as fake as he himself would soon have to act.

Chapter 8

Inside the Compound

Ghost grabbed Celeste's hand. *Just like old times.*
Dressed in the guards' clothing, they crept along the
hallway of the third level below the surface of the island. He
had to find Lydia if they had any chance to locate Django
and the Raptor.

"Do I have to wear this dead animal hat?" Celeste
whispered.

"Not unless you want to stay alive." He felt like a
Stranger in a Strange Land. "You won't see any women or
long-haired guards on the Raptor's payroll."

"Then how do you explain Lydia?" she asked.

"In the world of power and riches," he replied.
"Bloodline trumps philosophy. Besides, she doesn't wear a
uniform.

"Then, she's not that much different from me.

"Oh yes she is."

A black guard walked past and nodded in recognition. Ghost returned his gesture.

"At least I see some of my own kind," he said.

"Caribbean chocolate." She smiled. "I haven't seen any of mine though."

"Saltine?" He shot her a deadpan glance.

A blue orb about the size of a baseball turned the corridor in front of them, and floated their way. It whizzed by Ghost's head, then came in from behind like a dog sniffing for a scent.

Ghost grabbed his rifle by the barrel, then swung around and hit it like a baseball batter, sending it bouncing off the walls and screeching around the corner.

"Nice hit." Celeste chuckled. "Now do we run to first base?"

"Depends on what the defense gives us," he said.

Suddenly, an ear-piercing alarm sounded, and a mechanical voice squawked, "Security breach, security breach."

Celeste turned toward him. "Ok, great, now what?"

"Keep your cool," he said. "It might be just a coincidence."

"Yeah, no doubt," she replied.

Guards swarmed in the corridor, many still adjusting their uniforms as they scurried to some unknown destination.

Ghost stopped one of them. Do you know where Lydia is?" he asked.

The man stared back. "Do you mean The Redeemer? No one calls her Lydia."

"Yes, my mistake." He looked down. "Too familiar."

"She's probably in the command center where she usually is." The guard broke loose from his grip, and hustled back toward his muster point.

Celeste's eyes widened. "The Redeemer?"

Ghost motioned for her to follow him toward the elevator. "I remember her saying something about level five," he said.

"Good memory," she said. "All I remember is a knockout body and cool shoes."

They found the elevator, and Ghost pushed the third floor button. The adjacent plaque read: Command Center. Apprehension mounted in his belly, but he had to be confident for Celeste.

The door opened. Guards hustled in both directions. The wall postings indicated command was to the right.

Sweat dripped into his eyes.

"Stay close," he said. "They know more than we do."

"Ya think?" She wiped her hand across her forehead. "This goofy hat is starting to stink."

"Shhh, stay focused. I'm going to need your presence of mind in a little bit."

Black and yellow postings announced: *Authorized Personnel Only*. Each passing warning sign felt like a hand closing tighter around his throat.

He glanced at Celeste. "You ready?"

"I guess as ready as I'll ever be," she said. "Good thing for all the yoga classes, because the art world didn't train me for this."

The corridor jagged a degree to the right. At the end of a short hallway they arrived at the entry to the command center. It required iris and fingerprint checks to get through the massive steel door.

Celeste wrinkled her nose. "Crap, " she said. "You'd think they'd be a little friendlier."

"Let's wait a second," he replied. "I really don't want to use this bad boy." He pointed to the butt of his rifle.

The pad started flashing colors, and the hinges creaked. Someone was coming through. He motioned that they move to either side of the doorway where he stood at attention. She did the same. As soon as the last guard had exited, he peeked around the casing, then caught the door just before it closed.

Hustling in, they were now inside an airlock, encased on both ends by steel doors.

"This is the way they usher you in to see Da Vinci's Last Supper," she said.

"You better pray this is not ours."

He examined the door they had just come through. Maybe there was a clue to the operation of the next one.

With a rush of air, it opened abruptly. Lydia stood facing them. Dressed head to foot in black, she looked like a ninja fighter.

"Welcome," she said. "I've been waiting for you.

Chapter 9

The Conference

The limo ride from the airport through the hot dusty
streets of Tehran tossed Django like an afternoon sail on
San Francisco Bay when the winds howled through the
Golden Gate. It seemed like the driver had been in a hurry to
get the Raptor and him to the mosque on time. Only in this
case, it was the Presidential Palace where the military
leaders of the Islamic world had gathered to hear their chief
arms dealer speak.

Guards covered every exit. Security cameras hung
below the crystal chandeliers and continuously swept the
room. How the hell was he ever going to escape?

Django rubbed the knot on his temple, and then turned
to the Raptor, who sat next to him at the immense
conference table. "Why do they keep referring to you as
Mudarris?" he whispered behind his hand.

"It's a sign of respect. It means teacher," he said.

"Under the circumstances you would do well to call me that, or Mohammed."

Django glared back. "Okay, Mohammed, and who am I?"

The Raptor paused. "You shall be called the Servant of Allah."

"Get outta here." Django sat back in his seat. "Really."

There wasn't much else he could do besides watch the proceedings. Glancing around the room, he noticed the carafes of tea on the white pressed linen, and name cards in front of each man. Some were dressed in traditional Muslim garb, some in suits. Representatives from China, Russia, and the Arab states surrounded the conference table. Even North Korea was there. This was some coming out party they'd thrown for Mohammed, the great teacher.

The Chairman, a vision in white from his turban and beard to his flowing gown, stood. "Gentlemen," he said. "Today is a momentous occasion. We are here to begin the journey of our prophesied victory over the forces of Satan."

As if on cue, the delegates rose in unison to applaud.

Django leaned toward the Raptor. "Say," he said. "You don't mind if I catch the remainder of this show in the head, do you? I got a little case of tourista."

The Raptor grabbed the wooden box lying between them, removed the Spear of Christ and pressed it against the top of the inlayed table. "You make a move, and I'll gut you like a pig."

"Good argument."

When the applause waned, the Chairman motioned for the gathering to sit.

"Gentlemen," he said. "May I present our friend, teacher, and deliverer, Mohammed Abraham."

The crowd jumped to their feet again.

Django reached for his water bottle. "I thought your last name was Goldman."

The Raptor rose to the cheers and waved like a rock star. He put his hand over the microphone and leaned down toward Django. "I have many names," he said.

Django swallowed a gulp of water. "Does Dickhead ring a bell?"

The Raptor cleared his throat, and gestured for his rabid followers to be seated.

"Comrades – brothers, we have arrived at a crossroads in history," he said. "Allah has provided for us the political climate and the means by which to claim His kingdom on earth. The day after tomorrow we will move on Jerusalem to reclaim the holy mount and establish a thousand years of peace."

The assembled delegates stood and cheered, reminding Django of a Giants game when there was a walk-off homer in the bottom of the ninth.

Django reached for the spear, but the Raptor beat him to it. He yanked it in the air for the crowd to see. They went nuts again.

"And with the Spear of Christ in my hand," he proclaimed. "Nothing on earth can stop us."

Holy mother of God. Django had to do something. It didn't matter that the spear was a fake, the Raptor believed in its power, and he was going to cause all hell to break loose if no one stopped him.

The crowd hit another crescendo of excitement. The Raptor laid the spear on the table and raised both hands in triumph. When he did that, Django grabbed the spear, leaped to his feet, then pressed the blade against the Raptor's neck. Automatic weapons clicked all over the room.

With the spear in his right hand against the Raptor's throat, he grabbed the microphone with his left.

"Put down your weapons," he yelled. "And give us safe passage out of the palace or I will slit your precious Messiah's throat."

"Shoot him. Shoot him," the Raptor screamed.

"No, master," a guard shouted back. "We will have our chance. Your safety is everything."

Using the smaller, older man as a shield, Django jerked

him backwards toward the hallway.

"You'll be dead before you get out of this room." The Raptor struggled to get the words out.

"Then so will you."

Django knew that tunnels criss-crossed beneath the palace grounds, but where was an entrance?

The Raptor reached into his coat pocket for the .38. Their hands collided. Django grabbed the gun, pulled it out, and held it against his hostage's temple. As they stumbled backwards, Django had to drag the much heavier man.

"Okay, Mr. All-knowing." He spoke in the Raptor's ear just above the headlock he had him in. "Now, how do we get to those tunnels?"

"So, Lucifer now wants to flee from the light?" His voice was choked but steady.

"Quit playing these idiotic games or we're both going to die." He tightened the grip around the Raptor's neck. "Do you understand?"

The crowd was now standing, silently gaping at the spectacle that Django directed. All the eyes and the rifles in the hall were trained on the two of them.

The Raptor gasped for air. "There – there's a flight of stairs – just beyond the portico that leads down to the basement." He coughed. "There are two doors at the bottom of the stairs. One leads to the tunnels."

Django turned quickly and spotted the door. The strain of no sleep, a pounding head, and the weight of the prophet of doom were wearing on him.

He reached the door and turned the handle. Once on the other side, he held the gun on the Raptor and jammed the spear between the door handle and the steel casing.

"That ought to hold them back for awhile," he said.

He motioned for the Raptor to precede him down the tiled stairway that now turned at a right angle.

"Where does this lead?"

"There's no way to know," the Raptor said. "The Iranians have been building tunnels for centuries. They have built another world down here."

"Great." Django tripped, but caught himself. "Is there communication with the surface?"

"They have sophisticated telecommunications," he said. "Never underestimate these people."

"Give me your cell phone," Django demanded.

"It won't do you any good," he answered coolly. "They will find you."

Django cocked the .38, then reached for the pocket where the Raptor carried his phone. He found it, but the awkward arm thrust caused him to lose his balance. He tripped and fell headlong down the stairwell. Tumbling in what felt like slow motion, he landed at the bottom in a heap.

When he gathered himself, the Raptor was gone. His back and neck felt like he'd been kicked by a horse. Nausea swelled in his throat. The landing smelled of urine and sweat. Still wobbly, he struggled to his feet.

As the Raptor had said, he faced two doors. In the dim light, he could make out a new-age magnetic lock on his left, while the one on the right had an ancient lock that looked like it came from a pirate's chest. *Now what?*

Above him, guards banged against the metal door. He only had seconds. Standing to the side, he fired a shot at the pirate lock. The echo was deafening. He hit it but missed the locking mechanism. The projectile merely swung the lock like a pendulum. In spite of the risk, he had to fire at it head on, from point blank range.

The metal door above him slammed open against the wall. The sound of hustling boots rang down the stairs.

Hoping the next bullet wouldn't ricochet, he moved close, and aimed. Did he protect his face, his stomach, or his groin? He covered his eyes with his left arm, and fired. The lock exploded. With ears ringing, he quickly patted around his body. No new wounds, no new pain, a sliver of hope.

He threw open the door, and then hobbled as fast as he could down the medieval tunnel. His right knee - weak from an old baseball injury - buckled. Corridors snaked off in every direction. Which one should he take?

He fought back a wave of sickness. What a hell of a way for it all to end: alone, lost and desperate, trapped beneath the most hostile city in the world.

Chapter 10

Caught

Ghost glanced at Celeste, then his attention flashed to the woman in front of him. He couldn't believe he stood face to face with Lydia, the queen bee of the island. Was it time for flight, or fight? Celeste was wide-eyed and frozen. The door slammed shut behind them. The only way down the narrow corridor was through the woman in black.

"So, you've been tracking us?" he asked.

Lydia put her hands on her hips. "Every move. There's not much I don't know about if it happens on this island."

Every muscle in his body was tense as he surveyed the walls and ceiling of the passageway for a course out of there.

"You don't say," he replied. "Then, I guess the uniform change was a waste of time."

"That's right," she said. "Not only did I know where you were, but also what you were thinking."

"How about now?" he asked.

She smiled. "Don't even think about trying to overpower me. You're outlined in a laser web that can destroy you at my discretion."

He took off the guard hat, and his dreadlocks fell onto his shoulders.

"So why didn't you eliminate us earlier?"

"I wanted to see what your plan involved."

"Innocent people could have died."

"There are no innocent people. People are expendable," she said. "Only ideas and land live on."

"Children aren't innocent?" He was angry now. "Soulless bitch," he muttered.

"Show me your soul," she said. "Why do you risk your lives for Django Roth? Is it wealth you're after?"

"Not me," he said. "I guess friendship is another emotion you don't get."

Celeste took her hat off, revealing her long auburn curls. "It's simple for me," she said. "I love him, and I want him back."

Lydia laughed. "Ah, love," she said. "The undoing of sentimental people."

Lydia pushed a button on her cell phone, and a cadre of guards materialized behind her.

"I have no more use for the two of you." She turned to

the guards. "Take them away and do what you want with them."

The guards moved in.

"Wait." Ghost walked toward her. The guards immediately seized him and snapped on a set of handcuffs.

"There's something you need to know," he said as he struggled against his bindings.

She spun around. "It better be good. I've run out of patience."

"The spear that your boss has is a fake."

Lydia's eyes widened. "Oh, really, my father has a fake relic?"

"Your father?" That was a shock. He'd seen the squat, homely Raptor online, and she was the direct opposite of that.

"Then, where is the real spear?" she demanded.

He glanced at Celeste. "We've hidden it."

Lydia rubbed her chin. "If you're telling the truth, which one of you do I torture to find it?"

He had to think fast. "First of all, the truth can be verified by carbon-14 dating, and second, it takes the two of us to make it work." He nodded toward Celeste.

Lydia scowled. "What makes you think I can't awaken the power?"

Since there was nothing to activate, she was right. He'd

matched wits with Celeste, but this woman was a different bird. With her command of the martial and psychic arts, and with his hands bound, and their lives at stake, he had to reach deep.

"It has to be activated by those who are trained in the mystical arts," he said. "It takes a trained male/female polarity to awaken the electromagnetic force."

Celeste raised her brow, and her forehead wrinkled.

Lydia sidled up close to Celeste, and stared at her deeply. Then, she moved over to him. He tried not to think about the lie he'd just told. Instead, he tapped his foot and focused on a drum rhythm. Lydia motioned for a guard to lift her so that she was eye to eye with Ghost.

"You're lying, but I'll play along for a very short time," she said. "You mask your thoughts well, but I saw a brief vision of the spear on the boat. We'll retrieve it, and then carbon-date it in our lab."

"What are you, clairvoyant or something?'

"Yes," she said, "As a matter-of-fact. Now, let's go. Time is the enemy. If what you're telling me is true, I have to get the spear to my father."

"And how will you do that?" he asked.

"We have a duplicate here of our Learjet my father is now piloting to the Middle East. I'm a fighter pilot, trained by the Iranian Air Force."

What didn't this woman know? He had to figure out a way to keep them alive, and get them on that jet.

They approached the boat with a company of guards following close behind. Rain stood at the bow of the boat, and growled.

"Easy, boy," he said.

Now wasn't the time to let him loose. The guards would cut his dog down before he could take out a single man.

"You sure this is the best way to handle this?" Celeste whispered through clenched teeth.

"Just follow my lead."

"Uh, yeah, like that's working so far."

Lydia shouldered her way between them.

"That's enough talking," she said. "I'll tell you when I want you to speak."

Ghost grabbed Rain by the fur of his neck and led him off the boat. The Lab resisted as if he knew he had something to protect. Once on the landing, Ghost spoke softly in his ear. Rain stayed on the dock. Ghost retrieved the spear underneath the rear seat, and then brought it to the group.

"What did you tell him?" Celeste asked.

"I told him to listen for my thoughts."

Celeste rolled her eyes.

Lydia grabbed the Spear out of his hands. She closed her eyes, and held it against her breast.

"There's something powerful here," she said. "It's full of vibrations and images."

"That it is." The Caribbean humidity and the thick uniform caused sweat to drip from his forehead.

"Well, impressionism isn't my expertise." Celeste unbuttoned her jacket. "I'm a realist."

Lydia motioned for them to move up the ramp. Ghost gave Rain the sign to stay, and then turned to the nearest guard.

"Feed and water my dog, will you?" he said. "He hasn't done anything to you."

The guard nodded.

"Silence," Lydia yelled, and glared at the guard. Then she turned to Celeste.

"You mentioned impressionism," she said. "You're an artist?"

"A painter, yes."

"Then we're going to take a quick detour on our way to the lab," she said. "I want to show you something."

Ghost eyed both of them. He wasn't sure what was happening, but he had to manage the situation somehow. Man, how he hated to leave his dog behind.

The elevator descended and then opened on the seventh

level to a large studio of working artists. Classical music drifted through the room. Track lighting illuminated a group that worked on paintings, each at a different stage of completion. He had a sense of déjà vu, like he had been there, or had seen these paintings somewhere before.

He turned to Lydia. "What is this?"

"The largest reproduction studio in the world," she said.

"I always wanted to see this place." Celeste walked closer to examine a painting.

"You what?" Ghost wasn't sure what he'd just heard. "You know about this place?"

"Uh, no." She looked uncomfortable. "You know I just love art."

Lydia put her arm around Celeste.

"How'd you like to help me?" she asked. "You scratch my back, and I'll scratch yours."

Ghost was handcuffed, bewildered, and now being played. Lydia was cozying up to Celeste, his dog was in the custody of a Raptor soldier, and their quest to find Django seemed to be slipping away.

He needed a beer.

Chapter 11

In the Tunnels

With each step he ran, Django's lungs burned hotter, as if the air was being sucked out of the tunnel. His brain told him they needed oxygen to operate the seemingly endless underground system, but he didn't even trust his own logic at the moment. He was in survival mode, knowing that his Iranian pursuers could be anywhere, and he had to find a way out – fast.

Limping down the corridor, he passed what looked like an army barracks. Another fork revealed a granary and food storage area. Making a right turn, an arms cache caught his eye. Then, he curved left into a corridor where he had to stop at a metal vault that covered the entire space. *What the hell was this?*

"A nuclear weapon vault," said a voice behind him.

Django spun and pointed the gun at the man behind him. He was middle-aged and looked more like a banker than a soldier.

"Did I say that out loud?" Django asked.

"Yes, you did," the man said. "That happens when one is alone with his thoughts."

"Who are you?"

"My name is Mehdi Faraz." He held up his hands and turned around. "As you can see I'm unarmed and not a danger to you."

Dressed in slacks and tennis shoes, his dark hair with gray around the temples touched the collar of his a wrinkled button-down shirt. He looked harmless enough.

Django held the gun steady anyway. "I don't trust anyone at this point."

"I don't blame you, neither do I."

"Then why did you approach me?"

"I've been following you. I suspected you were American, and when you spoke, I knew you were."

"And why would you trust me?"

"I wouldn't use the word trust," he said. "You were obviously running from something. I believe we may have a common enemy."

"You don't know anything about me." Was this guy hustling him?

"That's true," he said, "But I think we can help each other. Now, please put down your weapon. It makes me nervous."

The crash of a door echoed in the hallway.

Mehdi grabbed his arm. "Follow me. I know a place we can talk."

Django stumbled after the smaller man. Why should he trust this guy? For all he knew, Mehdi was just another crazy foreigner out to kill or rob him.

They ducked down a flight of stairs and entered another passageway that was tall, round, and looked to be coated in seamless white tile. It was wide enough for two full sized trucks to pass each other, and smelled of diesel fumes mixed with stale air.

"Stay close to the walls," Mehdi yelled. "The security cameras are focused on the roadway."

Django was losing ground. "How much farther?"

"Just a short distance. There is an air vent."

His knee was killing him. He felt like a wounded fugitive.

Mehdi disappeared into a hole in the wall. Django reached the opening and tried to follow, but banged his head on the top of the narrow tube.

"Ouch. Shit."

"I forgot to tell you to duck." Mehdi tried to suppress a laugh.

"So, you're a comedian?" Django rubbed the new bump

on his head.

They sat cross-legged facing each other in the middle of the circular air vent. There was just enough light emanating from above to illuminate the man's face.

Mehdi pulled his left foot over his right thigh and easily folded his legs into the lotus position. It was all Django could do stretch his legs out and lean back on his hands. He laid the .38 on the tile beside him.

"No, I'm not a comedian, I'm a journalist," he said, and then quickly looked around. "We can't spend much time here because they will locate us."

Django shifted his weight to his other butt cheek. "So why are *you* running?"

"I might ask you the same thing."

Django spun the .38 on the tile. "I've got the gun."

Mehdi smiled. "If my intuition serves me well, I think we are both running from this regime. Is that true? Now you tell me you're story."

As much as he didn't like to spill first, he had to talk to someone quickly if he was ever going to find a way out of there.

"I'm an American antiquities dealer. I have the true Spear of Christ, and I was in the process of selling it to Mohammed Goldman, or whatever his name is – I call him the Raptor – when he kidnapped me and flew me here to

Tehran and this crazy conference of bozos who seem to want to blow up the world."

Mehdi's mouth dropped. "Mohammed, the Raptor. Bismillah. In the name of all that is sacred, this man is an enemy of Allah."

"Well, duh. How do you know this?"

"As I told you, I'm a journalist, and a Muslim. I have been through many revolutions and purges since the Shah was overthrown in 1979. I know this man and his history. By the prophecy, we call this man Dajjal, you might call him anti-Christ."

"I call him an asshole," he said. "But why are they after *you*?"

"I come from a family of journalists – from before the days of the revolution. My parents both died - my father in prison under the Shah, my mother shot by the Ayatollah's gang. Our craft of reporting has always been censored by whatever government has been trying to manage our chaotic country, but it has gotten much worse since Ahmadinejad stole the Presidency in 2005."

"So, they are after you for publishing stories against the Islamic Revolution?"

"Yes and no. I stopped publishing above ground years ago. They are after me because of my Internet postings and my involvement with the student protesters. There are still freedom-loving people in Iran, and I have to tell their story to the world."

"Is your story that big of a deal?" Django had to adjust his legs again. "Government suppression happens all over the world."

"Yes, it does," he answered. "But we have no representation, no Amnesty International, nothing here to protect us, so we post and blog and hide. I do this for the children of Iran."

"Are there more of you?"

"Yes, many, but I don't know how many are still here. Most have left the country, been thrown in jail, tortured or are hiding like me, like an animal. We can't communicate with one another for fear of exposure. We live off the preparations."

Django scratched his head. "Preparations for what?"

"The nightmare war for which the government is planning."

"This place is way off."

Django leaned farther back on his hands and lifted his chin in order to crack his neck. He noticed something snaking down the shaft above him.

"What the hell is that?"

Mehdi scooted over to see what he was looking at.

"Let's get out of here," he said, and jumped to his feet.

"It's a camera."

Back at the main artery, they both stuck their heads around the corner. A flatbed truck lumbered slowly toward them. The two men in the cab appeared to be arguing. Both were gesturing wildly with their hands.

"Here's the plan." Mehdi said. "We'll jump on the back of that truck."

"They'll see us." He was sick of following other people's plans.

"No they won't. They're too busy fighting. You see that bulkhead between the bed and the cab window? They won't see us."

Django could barely hear him above the racket of the truck.

"Remember to sit in the middle of the back of the bed," Mehdi said. "That way they can't see us in their rear view mirror, and they won't be able hear us either."

As soon as the center of the truck was even with them, they ran to get up to speed. Django's knee was so stiff, he wondered if he could make it. Mehdi jumped on first and reached his hand out. Django stumbled, but Mehdi grabbed his arm with both hands and hoisted him on to the truck. They sat in the middle, touching shoulders.

"Where we headed?" Django asked. "And how do I get out of here?"

"Through one of the air shafts. They have ladders, but are hard to find. I know where many of them are."

"How do I find an opening if we get separated?"

"Too bad we don't have an Internet-ready phone. As paranoid as this government is about the cyber world, they have a secret GPS site for safety and their new recruits. Imagine that." He laughed.

"I have the Raptor's phone. It might be a smart phone."

"Let me see it."

Django reached into the vest pocket of his jacket, retrieved the cell phone and handed it to Mehdi who turned it on, pushed a few buttons, and then handed it back to Django.

"Just go to favorite places," he said. "It will be the first website listed. There is satellite communications down here, and it will show you a map and exit points."

The truck clanked noisily along the underground highway.

Django tried to massage the two knots on his head. "How extensive are these tunnels, anyway?"

"No one really knows. Some say tunnels connect the whole Middle East. We've heard that even the Israelis are burrowing under the Temple Mount in Jerusalem in order to destabilize our Dome of the Rock."

"Why would they do that?"

"To bring it down so that they can rebuild Solomon's Temple on that spot, and make Jerusalem ready for *their* Messiah."

"So, let me ask you," he said. "If all these warring religious factions are controlled by their respective prophets, would you do anything if you could stop this prophesied Armageddon?"

Before Mehdi could answer, the sound of gunfire and ricocheting bullets reverberated against the tile walls. Mehdi grabbed his neck. Blood spurted through his fingers, and he fell off the back of the truck.

Django jumped off and then cradled him in his arms. He was still alive, but blood erupted from his neck in rhythmic cadence. More gunfire broke his trance.

"Run," Mehdi gurgled. "Run in the direction of the truck – maybe another two hundred meters – on the left – look for an opening. Go. Go."

Gently, he laid Mehdi's head on the pavement, and then he ran like a trapped rodent. His shoes slipped against the slick tile. The cell phone bounced inside his breast pocket. The .38 swung wildly in his right hand. He prayed that he would find the opening before the sting of a bullet brought him down.

Chapter 12

Deadly Game

Celeste cringed every time Ghost grimaced with pain. She wondered why Lydia didn't feel compelled to handcuff her too. After all, she wanted to find Django just as bad, if not worse, than he did. They both had to get on that jet to Tehran with Lydia.

The afternoon sunlight spilled through the studio windows and washed the artists in an amber glow. Celeste and Ghost followed Lydia down an outside row of busy painters.

"Why don't you just take off his handcuffs?" Celeste pleaded.

Lydia scowled. "I don't trust him. He's too cunning."

"He can't do anything, and neither will I." She glanced outside. "Where are we going to run?"

"Neither of you has earned my respect," she said. "Why should I give you any freedom?"

The artists' studio was on ground level. On the field below, she watched people working out with a rubber orb whose size was slightly smaller than a child's bowling ball.

"You're probably right." Celeste looked for a psychological edge. "He might get the best of you."

"Excuse me." She bristled. "There is nothing either one of you could best me at."

"Care to wager?" Her prey nibbled on the bait.

Lydia put her hands on her hips and raised her chin.

"You have nothing to wager, and I already have the spear."

"True, but you don't know how to use it."

"Oh, you'll tell me, if you want to get out of here alive."

"I'll make you a deal," she said. "Let Ghost compete in that game they're playing out there. If he wins, then you take us to Tehran with you."

Lydia raised her eyebrows. "Ghost knows how to play ulama?"

"Maybe." She was bluffing.

"And what do I get if you lose?"

"We'll teach you the secret of the spear, right outside."

Ghost moved between them. "You two are talking about me like I'm not here. I don't know anything about ulama, Obama, yo momma. Just take these friggin' handcuffs off of me."

"Or what?" Lydia looked like she wanted a piece of his action.

Celeste grabbed Ghost's arm and glared at her. "Please, give us a moment by ourselves."

"Make it fast."

She pulled him to the side. "Will you just shut the hell up for awhile and let me handle this with her? You can do your macho man routine, uncuffed I might add, on that dirt out there that looks something like a soccer field. I know you're good at that. Or, do you want to continue trying to twist your hands off?"

"Are you crazy?" he asked. That's not football. You might just be digging a deeper hole for us."

"You've got to trust my intuition on this one. Your method hasn't exactly paid any dividends yet. You savvy?"

Ghost was steamed, but nodded.

They walked back to Lydia.

"He'll do it."

"Then let's get this match started," she said. "We're running out of time. The jet will be ready in minutes." They headed toward the exit. "You know this is the oldest sport in the Americas, at least 3500 years old. The loser in the ancient Mayan ritual lost his head."

Ghost ratcheted his head from side to side. "Yeah, well,

that ain't gonna happen, here."

"You'll do well. You're a good athlete." Celeste rubbed his arm.

"Oh yeah, the difference," he said. "Is that they're playing with gunship munitions. This looks more like dodge ball with a cannon ball."

Lydia grinned. "You'll get hurt a lot worse if you don't play."

Celeste recognized the playing field was modeled after the Great Ballcourt in Chichen Itza, in the Yucatan, but a slightly smaller rendition to fit the confines of the island flight deck. The vertical stone circles on either side of the court were closer to the height of basketball hoops, only sideways with a meager opening.

Ghost stood in one corner of the court and stripped down to his boxers. A Caribbean guard did the same in the other corner. They both donned leather loincloths. Leather pads dangled to their knees to provide protection from the 9-pound ball.

Celeste and Lydia took seats at center court. The platform was slightly raised above the playing surface. This must have been how Roman royalty felt at the Coliseum as they prepared to watch a bout between the Christians and the lions.

She didn't really know if Ghost could compete at this

sport, but at least the handcuffs were removed, and he looked pretty good stripped down to a loin cloth. She heard every sound the contestants made.

Ghost and his opponent met at center court and shook hands. The guard spit, narrowly missing him.

"I'm going to kick your ass," the player said.

Ghost managed to smile. "Not if it's just you and me, little man."

The referee rolled the ball down the centerline. The guard ran to it, slid like a base runner, and then hit it with his hip, sending it toward and then beyond Ghost's endline.

"One to nothing," Lydia yelled.

"What happened?" Ghost yelled back. "What's the point of this stupid game?"

"To stop the ball from going over your endline," Lydia said. "And then sending it over your opponent's endline. No hands. The game is to eight, and you're down one zip."

Ghost stared up, dumbfounded. The guard scored another goal.

"Two to nothing." Lydia seemed to be enjoying the mismatch.

"This is no contest," Celeste said. "You know he can't beat this guy. I thought it was more like soccer."

Ghost was beginning to get the hang of sliding to the ground and hitting the ball with his hip. Now sporting strawberries on both thighs, he was able to stop the hard ground shots, until his opponent starting lofting the ball in the air.

The rubber projectile rebounded with a hard carom off the man's right hip. It hit Ghost in the forehead, and he went down like a knocked-out boxer. The ball bounced off his glistening head and rolled over his endline.

Celeste jumped out of her seat and tried to head for him, but Lydia grabbed her arm.

"No one can go onto the court, except as a substitute, or until the game is over. Are you volunteering as a sub?"

"I can't play that game."

"Then stay put and watch this delicious spectacle."

Ghost struggled to his hands and knees. Blood dripped into his left eye. He stood up and shook his head.

"Three to nothing," Lydia yelled.

"Wait," Ghost hollered back. "What's that stone circle for?"

"The game is to 8, unless a player can't go on, or unless one of you puts the ball through the circle."

Ghost stared at the small hoop above his head.

Celeste glared at Lydia. "You are a mean, rotten bitch."

"Maybe, " she said. "But I can play nice too."

"I can't imagine it."

Ghost let one dribble through his legs, and the score

was four to nothing.

"As I told you before," Lydia said. "If you cooperate with me, I can make it much easier for both you."

"And what would that be?"

"Well, in case you don't know, my father is in the Middle East on a mission that could be life threatening."

"Yes, go on."

"It's possible that he may not return, and I could inherit this island and all the business ventures. I know how to deal arms and move assets, but I know virtually nothing about art, even less about the counterfeiting of it."

"So, what's that got to do with me?" she asked.

"I may need a partner, and I know that you are intimate with this trade."

"How do you know that?"

Lydia rubbed her hands. "Shall we just call it intuition? I know some things about you. Perhaps we have a secret bond between us females."

Ghost dove for a ball that raced toward the goal just inside the out-of-bounds line. He slid across the dirt, scraping the right side of his face, but missed the ball.

His opponent pointed and laughed. "What a pussy."

"Five to nothing," the guard yelled.

Celeste faced Lydia. "What's in this offer for me?"

"Half the profits and a trip for you and Ghost to see

your boyfriend."

"Both of us, right?"

"That's right, but you also owe me the secret of the spear."

She hesitated long enough to consider the consequences. "Okay, it's a deal."

They shook hands.

She stood and cupped her hands around her mouth. "Let's go." Game's over. We're going to Tehran." Then, she slammed her right fist into her left palm.

Ghost called his opponent to the centerline. He grabbed the man's head and slammed it into his knee. Then he picked up the ball, walked over to the stone circle, jumped up and slammed it through the hole. He picked it up again and held up both his hands in the gesture of a football touchdown. Strolling up to the dazed man, he dropped the ball on his slightly wrapped package.

"Here's the game ball, numb nuts," he said. "Keep the change."

Chapter 13

Internet Cafe

Django felt like he'd been running for days. His endurance was shot. The white corridors that trailed off into a vanishing point seemed like the recurring loop of a bad dream. Luckily, he found a toilet sign and hustled inside. He threw open each of the stall doors. No one was there.

After a much-needed pit stop, he washed the blood off his face, and then pulled the Raptor's phone from the breast pocket of his suit. He punched in favorite places, and a message popped up: "If you need a friend, go to neareasternantiquities.com." Good old Mehdi.

He found a map of the local underground system and the red dots that pinpointed the exit ladders. One was located out the bathroom door, to his right, then the first corridor to the left. He raced to the spot and found a ladder.

At the top of his long climb, he found a hefty manhole cover that somehow reminded him of the cables underneath the streets of San Francisco. He pushed and banged against the lid until it let loose from its steel casing.

After maneuvering it to the side, he climbed through the opening, only to emerge in the median of a busy Tehran intersection where horns blared, sirens wailed, and exhaust fumes choked his lungs. He coughed and staggered across the blacktop like the creature from the black lagoon.

Dodging cars, he ran to the curb. Small businesses lined the street. All the signs were in Farsi. He spotted one marquee that advertised in English that it was an Internet Café. He knew he was attracting the wrong kind of attention.

Once inside the cafe, he needed to get to a computer, find a friend, a familiar language, but especially make an effort to contact Celeste and Ghost.

The proprietor spoke to him in Farsi, further compounding his frustration. He shook his head and started to leave. The man came around from behind the counter.

"Wait," he said in English. "It's been so long since I've seen a westerner, I forgot how to behave. What do you need?"

Django knew there were spies everywhere, especially around a communications center. He had to make up a plausible story for this guy.

"Thank you," he said. "I'm a Canadian here on

business. I got separated from my associates when we stopped the limo for some kabob. I got lost in an alley and was mugged by some punks who took my passport, my money and my phone. I need to get online to find my group, but I'll have to pay you later."

The owner stared back in disbelief.

"We better call the police," he said. "This sounds like an emergency."

Django threw up his hands. "No, no, I want to handle this in a quiet fashion. Just let me get online and I can take care of this whole matter without a big hassle."

The man scowled. "Okay, five minutes."

Django rushed to a computer and typed in the URL Mehdi had left on the Raptor's cell phone. The website was indeed an antiquities address that looked similar to the ones he visited for business.

He registered, signed on as Freebird, and then posted a message: "Looking for a friend in Tehran."

Then, he a sent a note to Ghost's satellite phone: "Where are you guys? I'm free at the moment on the streets of Tehran. I have the Raptor's sat phone @ +881.549.6741. Don't know how long it will last. Need the cavalry."

A response popped up on the antiquities website: "What kind of a friend are you looking for?" It was from someone named Pari.

He noticed the proprietor was calling someone. He had to move fast.

"A freedom lover," he wrote.

Quickly a message returned: "What kind of freedom?"

"Personal."

He looked over his shoulder again. The man was still on the phone, but now waved his hands in the air.

A reply came. "Are you underground?"

"I have been," he said.

"I am looking for someone." It seemed a little bold, but these were quick and desperate times.

"So am I," he wrote. "Who are you looking for?"

There was a pause, as if the person was thinking, then, "Mehdi Faraz" came across the screen.

Holy mama, was this a setup? He knew that Mehdi had been a significant player in the underground movement, and the regime also knew that. What better way to flush out the activists? Yet, he had to take a chance. How much more danger could he be in?

"I was just with him," he wrote. "He has been mortally wounded."

"Where are you?"

"In an Internet Café somewhere on a busy street in Tehran."

"Do they speak English? Are there English signs?"

"Yes."

"What do you look like?"

"I have long black and gray hair tied in a ponytail, same colored beard and a rumpled black suit."

There was a pause before the words appeared: "I'm sitting three seats to your left."

Django pushed back his chair, so did the burka-clad Iranian woman three seats down. He smiled and tried to read her eyes as she approached. She pulled up a chair and sat next to him as if she were studying something on his screen.

"Are you American?" she whispered.

"Yes I am."

"We have to get out of here. The police will be here any minute."

Approaching sirens bleated in the distance. The proprietor moved to the doorway.

She turned and put her face close to Django. "Listen closely. Find the Milad Tower. It is the tallest building in the city, about three kilometers south. Stay in the shadows when you get there, and I will find you. And turn off your phone for God's sake, they're tracking you."

He started to speak, but she put her finger to his lips, and then hurried out the door. The sirens intensified. Django got up to follow her, but was blocked at the door by the owner.

Django stiffened. "I told you that I will pay you after I meet my friends."

The man grabbed both his arms. "No, you will wait here for the authorities."

Django struggled with him until he could break free. Then, he pushed the man to the side, and ran what felt like south. He hoped it was the right direction, or at least somewhere off the main grid, somewhere through the dark shelter of this dangerously new, ancient Persia.

Chapter 14
The Raptor's Encounter

The desk the Iranians had provided him was hardly suitable for the man who would bring peace to the world. After all, every prophet had to spend some time in the wilderness of the skeptics before his final bestowal. At least he had the spear, and he was confident the Revolutionary Guard would find Django before he had to leave for Jerusalem.

The black telephone rang.

"Father?"

"Yes," he said. "Lydia, where are you?"

"I'm on my way to Tehran with the true spear and Ghost and Celeste. They can invoke its power."

"But I have the spear in front of me," he said.

"No," she said. "You have a counterfeit. I have the real one. We have carbon tested it."

Static made her difficult to hear.

"I can't make out all your words," he said.

"Never mind," she said. "I will meet you at the private lounge at the Tehran airport in about five hours."

He lost the rest of the transmission.

Then, the red phone rang

"Is this Mohammed Goldman?" the male voice asked. It was Meir, the top operative in the Israeli Mossad.

"Shalom," he replied. "Are we ready?"

"Shalom. Yes, the weapons will be ready in the Kidron Valley just below the Mount of Olives, in an Israeli Army vehicle at 0800 day after tomorrow."

"Perfect."

"But I need your assurance that we will be able to start immediately on the Temple after the destruction of the Dome of the Rock."

"Of course," he said. "I have given you my assurances. What more do you need?"

"I need Lydia for collateral. We'll need her in exchange for the armaments."

This was crazy. "I can't do that."

"You must if you want our cooperation."

"Those demands are too steep."

"Rightfully so," he said. "With great honor comes great sacrifice."

"You're asking too much."

"Take it or leave it."

The Raptor paused to consider the enormity of exchanging Lydia for Israeli protection and weapons. His daughter was dearer to him than his own life. The options at this point were limited, and these were monumental circumstances.

"Alright," he said. "But you will give her back as soon as the operation is complete, correct? And you will guarantee my safe flights in and out of Jerusalem?"

"Of course," he replied. "I will need one other thing."

"What is that?"

"The spear."

"You must be joking."

"I am not."

The fake spear offered the Raptor some negotiating room, but he still needed to be convincing. He needed to demonstrate his resolve to a higher power.

"I can't do that," he said. "You must know the legend, that when the owner loses control of the most powerful talisman on earth, he dies."

"Yes, I've heard that myth. You have nothing to worry about. We'll also give the spear back to you when we both have achieved our goals."

The Raptor picked up the spear and ran his thumb across the blade. "You drive a hard bargain, but I have no other choice but to accept."

"Excellent. The exchange will occur at 0800 day after tomorrow in the Kidron Valley directly below the Golden Gate to the Old City. Shalom."

"Shalom."

He leaned back in his chair. Even if the worst happened, Lydia could escape from any situation. Exchanging the phony spear for infinite glory was a small price to pay.

There was a knock at the door. Without an invitation, a high-ranking officer of the Revolutionary Guard entered his office.

The Raptor stood and approached the man. "Sir, I beg your pardon."

"I was listening to your conversation with Meir," the official said. "And I take exception."

They stood face to face in the middle of the room. The Raptor had the spear in his hand.

"What exception?" he asked.

"So what are you, Mohammed? A Christian, a Jew, a Moslem? You're either with the revolution, or you are against us. Right now I'm inclined to believe you are an enemy of Allah."

The Raptor held the spear at his side, as he looked the man in his eye. "I answer to another power."

The official grabbed the spear out of the Raptor's hand and then used it to slice open an envelope. "I have an indictment I have to read to you."

The Raptor was stunned. "An indictment? For what?"

"For spreading mischief in the land and crimes against the Islamic Republic."

"You have no proof of that charge," he said.

The officer smiled and held up a mini cassette tape. "I have your conversation with the Mossad infidel. This alone will bring the death penalty."

Although he had plans to bring peace to the world through unconventional means, he had no intention of necessarily harming the Iranian state. He could not let any common man stand in his way.

The officer placed the spear on the table and turned to leave. The Raptor grabbed the spear and then from behind, plunged it into the man's neck. He twitched for a moment, then gurgled and fell dead at his feet.

He dragged him into the coat closet, wiped the blood off the tile, and sat back at his desk. Then, he picked up the red phone.

"Leatherneck?"

"Shalom," answered the voice on the other end.

"I'll meet you on the Mount of Olives at first light day after tomorrow."

"Roger that," came the reply. "Victory will soon be ours."

Chapter 15

Running with Anahita

Django nearly jumped out of his suit when she tapped him on the shoulder. Tehran was crazy enough without someone dressed like a ninja nun sneaking up on him.

"Hey, easy," he said.

"That *was* easy," she replied. "You're a little tense."

"I'm friggin' a lot tense," he said. "Can we get out of here? I feel like an agent of Osama bin Laden."

She grabbed his arm. "Don't worry. My people have seen everything. Most are happy the Americans finally assassinated him. Come. Follow me."

He quickly scanned the building and the street. "This place is insane. If the cops don't get me, these drivers will. How can they ignore stop signs? Where we going?"

"To my apartment. It's safe there."

"What's your name?" he asked.

She turned her partially hidden face toward him.

"Anahita."

They hopped on an orange city bus, which took them south, away from the Milad Tower and the mountains. He tried to blend in with the other passengers who seemed to know where they were going.

After a ride across town, dodging an array of taxis and motor scooters, the bus stopped in front of an older apartment building. Several young children with their mothers milled in front. They dashed up to the second floor and entered her unit. Inside, two young men jumped to their feet in unison. The haunting music of Googoosh filled the room.

"It's alright," she said. "He's a friend of Mehdi. Stand down."

The men sat back on the couch to watch an Al Jazeera news report. The apartment was strewn with books and posters of revolutionaries. He recognized some of the men, but only one of the many photos of middle-eastern women. Neda Agha Soltan, who was gunned down during the 2009 election protests, smiled in suspended innocence. Green banners hung from every wall. The book, *Lolita in Tehran*, lay partially open next to the computer.

She motioned for him to sit beside her at the PC. She removed her black chador from her head and body to reveal a striking, shapely brunette with brown, piercing eyes, dressed in a loose green top and fashion jeans.

"We have to get something straight," she said, and sat beside him. "Are you a spy for anyone?"

He straightened his back in the uncomfortable chair. "Like I told you, I'm an American businessman. Nothing more."

She glared at him. "If you are lying, I can't begin to tell you what these people might do to you."

"I thought your Green Movement was non-violent."

"We believe in such principles," she said. "But even we have our limits with traitors."

"I feel the same."

She typed in alkasir.com, and the website popped up on the screen.

"What's that?" he asked.

"It circumvents website censorship. This regime meddles in everything, but we have a few options now."

"I understand."

She gestured with the open palms of her hands toward the computer. "I want you to contact someone you know online and conduct a brief conversation with them."

"Why?"

"So that I can determine if you are telling the truth. I prefer text or IM because we can't afford the time for an email response."

He remembered Ghost's satellite phone number. Hoping his friend had it turned on, he sent a text: "Django to Ghost." Then, they both sat back and waited.

"Why do you do this?" he asked. "What are you fighting for?"

"The same thing everyone fights for," she said. "Freedom from tyranny."

Al Jazeera news showed troops and tanks gathering around the borders of Israel. The broadcast cut to the Oval Office in the United States. Drowned by the voice of the Farsi interpreter, the President's message was garbled.

"So, who are your allies?" he asked.

"We don't identify with any state or political movement. We distrust all governments and religions, except the true voice of conscience, and Allah."

His back felt twisted and he tried to stand, but she blocked him with her arm.

"Don't move too fast," she said. "While this revolution is non-violent, there are certain elements that are armed, and these young men are part of that."

He exhaled deeply. "Who's leading this revolt against the government?"

"Mostly women," she said. "The most oppressed minority in our country. We have perhaps the oldest continuous civilization on earth and women are still struggling just to be."

A box on the screen popped up: "Django, is that really you?"

"It's me, buddy," he typed. "I'm in a safe house in Tehran. Where are you?"

After a slight pause: "Celeste and I are on a Learjet in the Mediterranean with Lydia. Looks like east of Sicily. We have the real spear and are set to rendezvous with the Raptor at Khomeini International Airport in Tehran."

He looked at Anahita. "Is that good enough for you?"

"I need this Ghost person to identify what you do."

"Ghost," he typed. "What do I do for a living?"

"Have you lost your mind, fool?"

"No, I need you to verify my identity for my host."

"You are Django Roth, an idiot who travels around the world buying and selling art and ancient artifacts."

He started to type, but Anahita grabbed his hand. "Where are you from?" He felt her eyes burn into the back of his head.

He took his hands off the keyboard and turned to her. "I was born in the back of a psychedelic bus, on the road with the Hog Farm commune," he said. "But my belongings have spent most of their life in Berkeley California. I don't know if he knows that."

"Ask him," she said.

"Where was I raised?"

"Berkeley is all I know," came the reply.

He raised his eyebrows and looked at her again. "Satisfied?"

"No," she said. "Ask him where you were born."

"OK, compadre," he typed. "Where was I born?"

Another pause, then: "This is Celeste. I don't know who's making you jump through these flippin' hoops, but his name is Django Roth. My name should be Celeste Roth, and he was born in a bus with a roving band of gypsies and he hasn't been normal since."

"Okay," Anahita said. "Schedule your meeting."

"What time and where can we hook up?" he typed.

"We'll meet you in the lobby of Khomeini Airport at 5:00 p.m. local time."

"Roger that," he said. "Love you guys."

Someone banged at the apartment door. From out of nowhere, the two young men stood with AK47s facing the entrance. The good-looking dude threw a set of car keys toward Anahita. She pocketed them, grabbed the flash drive out of the computer, and then bolted for the balcony.

Django was already on the move toward the glass slider. "How'd they find us?"

"They must have been on our trail," she said. "I don't know how, but I do know they want to kill both of us."

She jumped over the railing and shinnied down the metal support post. "Move it."

He hit the ground running after her. "You people are not right."

They ran to a red Paykan car in the parking lot. A burst of automatic weapons fire exploded from the building behind them. They jumped in and she started the car.

"What the hell are these guys so pissed at?" he asked.

"Beauty," she said. "This whole regime is about control, and they can't control what women do to their emotions."

"What about your two friends in the apartment?"

"We sacrifice." Tears rolled down her face. "The handsome man was my lover."

They sailed through the smoke, out of the lot, and into the busy street, toward the oncoming sirens and flashing lights. He could only hope she knew a safe route to the airport.

Chapter 16

Encounter at Khomeini

Mohammed tapped his fingers on the desk of the console. Beside him sat the Chief of Security of Khomeini International Airport. With no one else in the room, they studied the bank of monitors in front of them, scanning every face in the crowd. His backup Learjet, with Lydia in the pilot's seat, had landed, but he hadn't located her yet. As soon as saw her on one of the monitors, he would order a Revolutionary Guard to retrieve her.

"You understand," he said to the Chief. "We're looking for my daughter, accompanied by a tall black Belizean man and a brunette American woman, right?"

"Describe your daughter, please," the Chief asked.

"She is Palestinian, maybe five foot three or four. Dark hair. Pretty. She'll be dressed in black."

The Chief tilted his head. "You do know we're in a security lock-down at the moment."

"I gathered that," he said. "Is it because of the impending war with Israel?"

"Partially. We *are* on heightened alert because of that," he replied. "But the actual triggering event is this. About forty-five minutes ago a man walked through a screening checkpoint into a restricted zone."

"Is that why there are so many people clogging the terminal?"

"Yes it is," he said. "We don't know what's going on at the moment, so we are suspicious of everyone. We're restricting all movement."

Mohammed tugged at the collar of his shirt. "Is the air conditioning on in here?"

"It's malfunctioning at the moment. I'm sure it will be repaired soon."

"I don't want my daughter to have to endure any more trouble," he said. "She's carrying a valuable package that I must retrieve."

The Chief turned to look him in the eye. "We have more pressing issues than retrieving a package from your daughter."

Mohammed felt his face flush. "Do you have any idea who I am and what I could do to you?"

"Sir." His tone was respectful. "I only know that you have the highest of security clearance, but we have an emergency and that takes precedence." He punched number one on the speed dial of his cell phone, and then turned his back to him.

Mohammed started to rise out of his seat, but, on the right center monitor, he spotted Lydia walking near the baggage area, between Ghost and Celeste.

"There she is," he shouted.

The Chief was talking on the phone, paying no attention to him or the monitors. Mohammed starting pushing buttons trying to enlarge the screen. One of the switches activated a high-pitched warning siren. The Chief reached across him, scrambling to shut off the alarm.

On another monitor, in main terminal, guards frantically gestured for everyone to hit the ground. The only people left standing, beside the guards, were Lydia, Ghost and Celeste. He knew the armed Basij would fire on anyone that moved.

The Chief couldn't shut off the alarm, and quickly exited from the control room. Mohammed's attention was drawn to another screen on the left where he recognized Django enter the terminal building with a Middle Eastern woman in a green blouse. *What was he doing here?*

He turned back to the right screen where Lydia was on the floor, but Ghost and Celeste were frozen in place, staring toward the automatic doors.

He ratcheted his head between screens, as Django and Celeste seemed to find each other across the terminal. They both threw up their hands, seemed to yell, and then began to run toward each other. The sound system speakers picked up the crack of gunfire, followed by screams. Passengers jumped to their feet and ran in all directions.

The Chief flew back in the security door. "What did you do? I can't shut off the emergency warning system."

Mohammed put up his hand. "Get someone down there to help my daughter," he demanded.

The Chief had the phone cradled to his ear as he jotted notes. "I'm sorry, sir, I can't do that right now."

Mohammed grabbed the telephone base and slammed it into the side of his head, driving the Chief to the floor.

"That will teach you to never disobey my command," he said as he stood over the dazed man. Then, he turned back to the monitors.

Within the chaos he spotted Ghost, then Celeste, but Lydia was nowhere to be found. He turned back to the groaning man to retrieve the handset. When he bent over, the Chief stabbed him in the right eye with his pen. He screamed, put his hand to his eye, and then pulled back a blood-drenched hand. Gripping the base like a shot put, he hit the man in the face again and again and again, until he was lifeless.

He tore off the man's coat, then ripped a sleeve from his shirt and tied it awkwardly around his head. Then, he punched the 0 on the handset, now slippery with blood.

"We'll need an emergency doctor on the number one Belizean Learjet, stat," he said. "Find Lydia Goldman in the concourse, and have her and the jet ready to leave for Jerusalem within the half hour."

He grabbed the Chief's cell phone out of the discarded coat's breast pocket, then he tore off the other shirtsleeve of the dead man. He wiped down the console and both pieces of the phone, then exited, locking the door behind him.

Holding his hand over the sleeve pressed against his bloodied eye, he stumbled toward the tarmac. He hit number one on the speed dial of the Chief's cell phone.

"Yes," a voice answered.

"This is the Chief," he said. "Have *one* guard bring the tall, black Belizean named Ghost to Learjet Number One, along with the woman, Celeste, who will be with him. Never mind if they have papers or not. I will take care of the rest."

"What about Django Roth?" the voice asked.

"Do what you will with him," he replied. "His value is nil."

The illuminated path stretched toward his private gate, although he didn't expect the fulfillment of prophesy to manifest in such a painful fashion.

Chapter 17

Reunion

As soon as Django spotted Celeste across the concourse floor at Khomeini International, a wave of affection washed through him, followed closely by a dread that something was terribly wrong. Everyone except Celeste and Ghost were sprawled on the tile. Guards everywhere were ready to fire.

He ran toward her, and she toward him. As they were about to embrace, he tackled her around the waist, and tried to bring her gently to the ground.

Still in his arms, she groaned. "It's good to see you, too."

He held her head to the floor, and gazed sideways into her eyes. Then, he kissed her with his best soul suck. "Situational awareness has never been your long suit, babe. Do you see these guys who are about to blow our brains out?"

"I see them," she replied. "But, I thought it was more important to get to you."

"I rest my case." He couldn't help but smile. Big reason why he loved her.

"And who is that?" She pointed to the woman who lay on the ground next to them.

"Her name is Anahita, and she saved my life. I owe her."

Celeste pushed his hand off her head. "Owe her what?"

"A chance at life."

He reached across Celeste's body to give Ghost a handshake. Gunfire filled the air. People started running and screaming.

Anahita jumped up. "Follow me."

They hurried across the expanse of the terminal building, dodging frantic passengers and nervous-looking guards. Django wondered what kind of attention they were attracting and where Anahita was leading them. He held Celeste's hand. Ghost was right behind them, protecting the rear.

"Where's the spear?" Django had to raise his voice in order for Celeste to hear him above the commotion.

"Lydia has it, but we lost her in the free-for-all," she said.

He had to push a wild-eyed passenger away from them.

"And the Raptor still has the copy?"

"Yep," she said. "You don't have either one."

"I can't live with that."

"You've got to give up on getting them back," she replied. "It's not worth any of our lives."

He gritted his teeth, knowing the volume of souls that were lost over the centuries in pursuit of the power of the spear, but this wasn't the time or place to debate that. Escaping with their lives eclipsed everything.

Anahita ducked into a corridor, and they followed. Then, she took another route that seemed to lead toward the tarmac.

"Are you sure this is the right way?" His sixth sense of danger was kicking in.

She motioned for them to hug the near wall. "Ironically, the least guarded area is closest to the main security room. Stay here while I check it out."

She peeked around the corner, then came back to the group. "There's a bunch of security people talking to a woman dressed in black."

Celeste squeezed Django's hand. "Lydia," she whispered.

"Can you understand what they're saying?" he asked Anahita.

"Let me see." She tiptoed back to the intersection of the

two walls and then crouched low.

Ghost tapped Django on the shoulder. "You know, I convinced the Raptor that he needs Celeste and me to invoke power of the spear."

Django had to stop the voices competing for his attention, and think for a second. "That's our advantage."

Celeste stared at Django and then grabbed Ghost's hand. "The three of us are in this together." Then she gestured toward Anahita who was still listening to the conversation between Lydia and the officials. "I don't know about her."

Django looked toward Anahita. "She can't stay here now either."

Celeste frowned.

Anahita walked toward them again. "It seems like the Chief has been killed in some kind of a fight, and that a guy named Mohammed may be implicated."

Django started to walk toward the spot where Anahita was listening. Celeste grabbed his arm. "What are you doing?"

"I have to verify if it's Lydia and that they're talking about the Raptor."

Anahita stood in his way. "You don't understand Farsi."

He shook them both off. "But I understand faces and

body language."

When he got to the spot he ran into Lydia coming the other way with her cell phone up to her ear. He struggled with her. Ghost ran to them, put her in a headlock and then gagged her with his bandana. They dragged her farther down the corridor.

"Take off your bra," Django said to Celeste. He was out of breath.

"What in the world for?" she asked.

"Just trust me," he said. "Hurry up."

Celeste shrugged and took off her bra without removing her blouse. "Here," she said.

With the bra Django tied Lydia's hands behind her. Anahita quickly removed her own bra and tied Lydia's feet. Then, they dragged her into a nearby restroom and he locked the door behind them. He grabbed her cell phone and listened.

He heard the Raptor's voice. "Lydia. Lydia. What's happening? Where are you? You need to come to my jet, ASAP. There's no time to lose."

"Now listen, and listen closely," Django said. "We have Lydia, and I have your .38. We'll kill her if you don't cooperate."

"Roth you miserable son-of-a-bitch," he yelled. "I'm going to get off this plane and come and strangle you with my bare hands. I should have killed you when I had the chance."

"Oh really? You get off that plane and you'll immediately be arrested for the murder of the chief."

"What the -?"

Django interrupted him. "The only chance you have is to fly to Jerusalem like you planned and then arrange with whatever protection you have to allow your other plane with five people aboard to land right behind you."

"I'm going to kill you."

Django paused to look at the people he loved, and at his squirming hostage.

"No," he said, calmly. "You're going to pay me. Oh, and you better hit the runway before it's too late."

The roar of Jet exhaust drowned the Raptor's response.

Chapter 18

Flight to Israel

Django sat in the co-pilot's seat and adjusted the volume on his headset. In the pilot's seat, Lydia followed the instructions from the control tower. This would be a piece of cake as long as they stayed in contact with the Raptor's jet, and maintained a safe separation. He would breathe a little easier when they were in the air.

The plane swished by the control tower, gathering speed. The Raptor's jet floated in the sky in front of them.

"You know, your lives are in my hands." Lydia's voice crackled in his ears.

He looked at her. "It's your life, too."

As they climbed through the cloud cover, he glanced around to see that Celeste, Ghost and Anahita were safely in their seats. In an effort to calm their jitters, he flashed the okay sign. He'd put them through enough in the last day and a half. Jerusalem would be another story.

Lydia squeezed his balls. "The action is up here. Pay attention."

"Ouch," he yelled. "Stop that." He tried to adjust himself. "Pain is the wrong motivator."

"It works in interrogation," she responded.

"What a bitch."

Lydia reached over to slap him, but he grabbed her hand. As he restrained her hands, the jet dived. He heard screams from the back, and tried to grab the controls. Lydia went for his throat. He slapped her hard across the face. She went limp in the pilot's seat.

He grabbed the wheel and pulled the plane out of its steep dive. At least he could do that. The rest was a total mystery. He'd always enjoyed flight simulation games, but this was the real thing.

Celeste ran up to him. "What's going on?"

"See if you can revive her." He searched the instrument panel in front of him.

"What happened?"

"I think I knocked her out."

"You think you knocked her out? What the hell would you do that for? You can't fly this thing, and nobody else can either."

"It was an accident," he said. "She was trying to choke me."

"I know how she feels."

Django eased back on the throttle to lessen their air speed while he tried to figure out what to do.

She shook Lydia. Nothing changed. "I think she's breathing, but I can't bring her around."

He reached over and undid Lydia's harness. "Pull her out of the seat and lay her down in the back."

"I can't lift her."

"Get Ghost and Anahita to help you."

As Django tried the radio controls, they lifted Lydia from the pilot's seat and placed her in the rear cabin.

Celeste was out of breath when she returned. "Now what?"

"Strap yourself into that seat, and put on the headphones."

"What? Are you completely nuts?"

"Somebody has to assist me," he said. "Now, sit down and buckle up."

She sat and then struggled with the harness. "I don't even know how to do this."

"It's a five point system," he said. "Just go in a circle, and don't forget your crotch."

"You wanna help me?" she asked.

He'd sure like to do that, but he needed to get some help to keep them in the air, and if Lydia didn't regain consciousness, he'd need help to land. The Raptor was his only hope.

He keyed the radio. "Belize Learjet Two to Belize Learjet One," he shouted.

"Roth, is that you?"

"Yes it's me," he said. "I need your help. Over."

"You've got to be dreaming. Why on earth would I help you? Over."

"Because I'm right behind you in your other plane with your daughter who is passed out."

"Shit," he said. "What did you do to her? She has a heart condition."

Django looked at Celeste who was now listening in the headset. "We had a little accident."

"If you hurt her, I'll torture you."

"Screw that," he said. "If my calculations are correct, we're less than an hour from Jerusalem and I'll need to be talked down in this bird."

"Ok," the Raptor said, after a long pause. "But you do exactly as I say, and don't give me any lip."

"You got it," he said. "Just get us down safely."

"First, I'm not even sure we can land at Qalandia in Jerusalem. It's controlled by the Israeli military and not open for civilian traffic."

"Just get it done," he said. "And what if we get an

Israeli air force intercept."

"I'll get back to you when I've made arrangements. Just hold steady on your compass and reduce your speed to three hundred knots."

Django turned quickly to see what was happening. While Ghost attended to Lydia, Anahita walked toward the cockpit.

She put her hand on Django's shoulder. "They won't let me into Israel."

"None of us are kosher," he said. "Celeste is the only one who has a passport, and no one can fly from Tehran into Israel anyway. We have to rely on Mohammed."

The headset crackled. "Learjet Two, we can land. Punch JRS into NAV1 on your radio."

"Roger."

"Now hit the swirling gizmo next to that to activate it."

"I can't find it."

"You have to be down to at least 150 knots for landing and your vertical descent has to be about 750 feet per minute."

"I can't even lock in the airport."

Someone tapped him on the shoulder. When he looked around Ghost pointed to each wing. Israeli F16s shadowed them on both sides.

The plane was losing altitude too fast. He tried to make

adjustments. Ghost, Celeste, and Anahita were yelling at him and pointing. His head was spinning.

Someone's hands began unbuckling Celeste's seat belt. He turned his head. Lydia motioned for Celeste to get out of the pilot's seat.

Chapter 19

Bailout

Django peered out the co-pilot's window of the Learjet as Lydia steered the plane over the Dead Sea. The arid landscape didn't look any more inviting than the Iranian terrain he'd just left.

"Can you fly?" he asked Lydia.

"I'll make it," she said.

"You may not like me, but we're in this together."

"I don't like you," she said. "But we have more pressing matters now."

"I didn't think there was an airport in Jerusalem."

"Technically, the Atarot/Qalandia airport is inoperable," she said. "The Israeli's use it as a forward base for troops. It's a serious bone of contention in the conflict."

"It's in occupied territory on the West Bank, right?"

She flipped a switch on her instrument panel. "Yes, and after the second Intifada, the Israelis finally shut it down."

"Why the two names?"

"And two airport codes, one Palestinian, one Israeli," she said. "As far as I know the only one in the world." She turned to look at him. "Pretty good for a non-working airport, eh?"

"Really, then how are we going to land?"

"My father has made arrangements," she said. "I trust him, and he is very connected to the Mossad."

He turned in his seat to see if everyone else was sitting and buckled in. "I thought he was a Muslim."

"He is all things to all people."

"Oh, right, I nearly forgot." All Django knew for sure was that the Raptor was a pain in the ass to him. "Does this jet carry parachutes?"

"Actually we do carry a couple in the back compartment," she said. "But it would be futile. By the time you could get one on, it would be too late."

"You mean we're just stuck in here like sardines if something happened?" He stared out at the two F16s that shadowed them. "Like if one of these guys decided to bring us down?"

Lydia banked the jet to the left as she made her approach to Jerusalem.

"If the engine didn't suck you in, the bang against the wing would probably kill you. I'm not even sure you could get the door open in flight."

"So, there's no hope?"

She flashed a thin, wry smile. "Technically, I suppose it would be possible if the jet stalled, the speed was slow enough, and the five of us could squeeze into two parachutes."

He groaned. "Well, there goes that plan."

Celeste tapped him on the shoulder. "Could I have a word with you?"

Django motioned for Anahita to come and sit in the co-pilot seat. When she came to the cockpit, they exchanged places. Django squeezed her shoulder, then bent over to whisper in her ear. "Distract her for a second, " he said.

He dropped a pen behind the captain's seat. Anahita moved her hands quickly across the instrument panel. Lydia grabbed her hand and stared at her.

Django bent over behind Lydia. "Oops, sorry," he said.

He scooped up the spear Lydia had placed behind her seat, then he quickly stuck it inside his suit and down his leg, wedging it against his skin inside the pressure of his belt.

Anahita had Lydia pre-occupied. He walked to the salon and sat with Ghost and Celeste.

"What did you want?" he asked her.

"Is this relationship still paramount to you?"

"Of course it is."

"Then you have a decision." She stared him in the eyes. "I want you to give up this insanity."

He kissed her on the lips. "Soon. But first I have another plan. We have to move fast."

She shook her head. "Oh, I can't wait for this one."

"Do either of you know anything about this plane?" He searched both their faces.

"Actually," Ghost responded. "I have been in one of these rocket ships a few times with some high rollin' U.S. fisherman, and I've been reading the manual." He held up the documentation on the jet.

Django looked out the window to try to get his bearings. "Do you know how to control the throttle and the stick?"

"Well," he said. "I know where they are and how they function."

Lydia fine-tuned her approach to the airport.

"Okay," he said to Ghost. "I want you to change places with Anahita in the co-pilots seat. As soon as you do, you need to put the jet in a stall by pushing the throttle all the way off and pull back on the wheel as hard as you can.

Ghost's eyes widened. "And what are you going to do?"

"Bail out with the spear."

"What?" Celeste screamed it so loud, both Lydia and Anahita turned around.

Django waved and smiled as if to say that everything was okay. "There are a couple of parachutes in the closet. I'm going to strap one on, and when Ghost puts the jet into a stall I'm going to open the door and jump. Celeste, you may have to help me with the door if the pressure is too great."

She had her head down. "I will not watch you die or let you kill the rest of us."

"You have to help," he said. "It's the only way we can all get out of this alive."

Ghost rifled through the operating manual. "Now, how do you figure that?"

"If we land with the spear," he said. "The Raptor gets what he wants, you guys won't be able to fake an incantation, and he'll eliminate me. If he doesn't have me or the spear, we all stay alive, and we have a bargaining chip."

Celeste had tears in her eyes. "There are no guarantees in any of this."

He kissed her cheek and wiped her tears with his thumb. "Sweetheart, there's no guarantees in life. We've got a desperate situation, and time is running out fast."

Ghost studied the diagram of the instrument panel. "Have you thought about the speed, the altitude and all that, and how you're going to locate us?"

Django walked to the rear and found the parachutes.

"Yes," he said. "She has to land at about 150 knots or so. Our speed is rapidly decelerating. I can handle that. The cabin pressure is reaching a normal atmosphere, and I can make it if we stall and don't get below about two thousand feet."

"How do you know she can start this thing up again?' Ghost asked.

"She's a trained pilot. It's standard operating procedure." Django examined the parachute. "You guys stand in front of me." He strapped it on.

Ghost took a step, then turned. "It's a good thing I'm stronger than she is." He gave Django a bear hug. "Be careful, my brother. Find us quick. God speed."

Django squeezed him. "Keep your sat phone on."

Celeste who had her face in her hands, looked up. "I'm not going to let you leave me again."

"You have to, babe," he said. "It won't be for long, and it's the only way. Now come on and help me with the door."

Ghost started a commotion in the cockpit. Anahita ran to the back. "What the hell is going on?" she demanded.

"We're going to stall the jet, and I'm going to parachute out." He put his arm around her. "You're going to be all right. I'll catch up with you in Jerusalem. Everything will be okay."

"You know," she said. "If you, or any of us survives, you'll probably land in Palestinian territory. Then what are you going to do? I'm the only one who can help you."

The jet started a steep climb. They fell against each other. Then, the engines died, the plane leveled off, then the nose pitched downward.

"The door," he yelled.

The three of them pulled it open. He only had a second before Lydia would start the engines again. He turned, smiled at the two women, and cinched his belt tighter against the spear.

The wind buffeted his suit. He stepped out on the wing and dived off the rear. His legs crashed into the tailpiece and sent him tumbling end over end. The ground was rushing up too fast. He spread his limbs to try to stabilize, and then he searched for the ripcord. Where the hell was it? It had become entangled in his collar. He pulled it. Nothing happened. He pulled with both hands. His body jerked, and then, mercifully, the white sheet billowed above him.

Below him, what looked like a shantytown seemed to spread its arms in anticipation. Children gathered in the street, screeched, and pointed skyward. Where in the world was he going to land?

He looked up to try to find the jet. In the bright, burning sky, another parachute followed him down.

Chapter 20

Palestine Landing

Django aimed for the middle of the street. The closer he
got to the ground, the more he noticed the number of lines
that criss-crossed above and between the ramshackle
buildings. On closer inspection, he could make out
clotheslines, electrical lines and guy wires that seemed to
hold the buildings from collapsing.

He pulled on the chute to try to avoid the entanglement,
but as soon as his body flew past, the nylon got caught in
the web of wires. Dangling six feet off the ground, he
struggled to get free. Children jumped up to try and grab his
legs. Adults poured into the street. He grabbed the spear out
of his pants and cut his connecting chords, dropping into the
center of the crowd. The children ripped at the chute, and
ran off with the precious spoils as the adults pointed and
stared.

Then, he noticed blood soaking through his right pant

leg, then the pain. The tailpiece of the jet had cut a gash just above his knee, and it bled profusely. The jabbering throng was driving him crazy. He felt faint. What could he use for a tourniquet?

Anahita broke through the crowd and yelled in Arabic.

"Where did you come from?"

"Same plane you did," she said. "I just landed down the street where there weren't any wires."

"I thought Celeste had jumped."

"Why Celeste?" she asked. "She has a future. I would be deported or imprisoned as soon as we touched down at Atarot. Besides, you need me."

"What about the others? Are they okay?"

"I didn't hear a crash," She looked up at the sky. "I imagine Lydia got the jet started, and they're landing at Atarot about now."

"Can you get us out of here?"

She pulled up his pant leg. "You need immediate medical attention."

"Tie me off with something," he said. "We have to get to Western Jerusalem."

"You can't go anywhere until we get this bleeding stopped."

"Bullshit. These people look like they want to eat us or something."

The crowd pushed in tighter. Anahita grabbed one of the gawking man by the shirt yelled in his face.

Then, she turned to Django. "Let's go," she said. "We can get help at this man's house."

"Can we trust him?"

"At the moment, we have no other options."

They swam through the crowd toward the row of adobe and mud apartments. Garbage accumulated on the street in front of the structure's walls. They entered the man's dwelling. It was too impoverished to be called a tenement. He heard the cacophony of what seemed like hundreds of refugees living side by side and on top of each other, with nothing but imagination to distinguish one person or living space from another.

"I know what you're thinking," Anahita said. "Remember, the Israelis are an occupying force on these people's land, and they control everything. Americans don't see this side of the conflict."

"I know," was all he could manage.

One chair squatted in the single-room partition. There was a hole in the corner for a bathroom. He pulled the spear out of the back of his pants and laid it on the table. The man's wife flashed on the blade, then motioned for him to sit. Then she tore off the pant leg to examine his knee.

Django grimaced and looked at Anahita. "Is there any

way we can see a real doctor? Maybe in Jerusalem?"

She spoke to the man.

"He says there are no doctors available, and that it will take hours to get into Western Jerusalem, even if we could get in with no papers."

The woman cleaned, then wrapped his wound with muslin. Anahita squatted in the corner and conversed with the woman's husband. The rest of the half-dozen family members gathered, alternating their stares between Django and the spear.

Another Palestinian man burst in the door shouting and waving his hands.

"What's he screaming about?" Django asked. "I'm the one in pain here."

"He says the Israelis are bulldozing down his house next door."

The hysterical man spotted the spear Django had laid on the table. '

"What is that?" he asked in Arabic.

Anahita spoke to him.

"What did you tell him?" Django asked

"That it was a special antique."

He shook his head and exhaled deeply. "Oh man, that wasn't cool."

"The man asked an honest question," she said. "I gave

him an honest answer."

"I don't trust these people."

"You don't trust Arabs."

"It's not a racial or cultural thing," he said, shaking his head. "I'm just looking for an ally to get us the hell out of here."

The man grabbed for his cell phone to call someone.

Anahita looked distressed. "Oh, oh," she said.

Django looked around the room and into the street. "What?"

Within seconds, three Palestinian Authority guards blew through the open door.

Django jumped up. "What the hell is this all about?"

Anahita was already on her feet. "He told them we are IDF spies."

"Oh shit," he said. "Tell them we demand to speak to the American embassy."

She addressed them, and they laughed. "We're screwed," she said.

The Palestinian snitch pointed and screeched as the guards escorted them out of the apartment.

Django jerked his head around. "Don't forget, that spear is mine."

One of the guards grabbed it.

Outside, the man started screaming again, this time in

Django's face.

"What's he yelling about now?"

"He says you're a crusader asshole," she told him. "And he hopes they cut you up into little pieces."

Django grabbed the guy by the throat. The PA guards jumped in to break it up.

Anahita listened to his cries for a moment.

"The Jews say that he has no permit for his house. He's also apparently on their bad boy list."

"Bad boy list?"

"Yeah," she said. "They suspect he may be a terrorist."

"Perfect." He glared at the man. "I'm about ready to take this guy's head off."

The rumble of the bulldozer nearly drowned their voices. The street smelled like an open sewer. As the man's house was slowly reduced to rubble, he screamed, and picked up a handful of stones, then hurled them at the operator.

That act pushed Django over the edge. He broke free from the grip of the PA guards and tackled the agitator, causing the guards to jump into the fray on top of both of them. The Palestinian at the bottom bit, kicked and spit. Django was able to free his right hand. He landed a single punch square to the man's chin, silencing his screams.

The next thing he knew, military men were dragging

him across the dirt road, away from the house. But these weren't Palestinians, they were Israeli soldiers. Anahita struggled against the guards who were dragging her right along with him.

"How did these guys get here?" he yelled.

"They were protecting the bulldozer."

The IDF soldiers threw him and Anahita into an armored vehicle and sped away from the scene.

He sat upright. "Where are they taking us?"

"Ask them," she said. "My guess is they speak English."

"We speak English," the soldier told him. "We're taking you to the base for interrogation."

"We're the good guys," Django said. "The bad guys were throwing the rocks."

The soldier placed his weapon across his lap, but kept his finger on the trigger. "We know all about the Palestinians," he said. "It's you two we don't know about."

"Do you have my spear?"

"We have both your weapons. The sword and the .38 that dropped out of your pocket in the fight. The Katsas will be very interested in you."

"What is this Katsas, and where is it?"

"You might call him the Captain," He stumbled for the right words. "Oh why not, you will probably not see the light of day for a very long time. With the war about to break out, you are our first POWs."

Django locked eyes with Anahita. "That's nonsense. We're non-combatants. I'm an American businessman, and she's an Iranian student."

The soldier adjusted himself. "That just happens to be armed to the teeth in a combat zone."

"Where are you taking us?"

"To discuss this with the director of Mossad at Atarot Airport."

Chapter 21
The Demand

The trip to the Atarot Airport in the belly of the Israeli armored vehicle had been hot and bumpy. His pretzel-like posture in the cramped quarters hadn't helped the pain in his knee either. Now, waiting for the Mossad commander in the airless room with Anahita was working his nerves.

A tall, tan man in camouflage fatigues strode into the interrogation room. His thin black moustache was reminiscent of that of a World War II British commander.

"My name is Moshe Zamir," he said. "I understand that your name is Django Roth, an American businessman, who has been attempting to sell the Spear of Christ to Mohammed Goldman."

"How do you know that?"

"It's my job to know everything."

He turned his head. "And you are Anahita Tabrizi, an Iranian activist. Neither you nor Mr. Roth has a passport, which is against the law in Israel."

"I can explain," said Django.

"So can I." She chimed in.

Zamir waved his hand. "It doesn't matter. I'm totally aware of your circumstances."

"Then, I can have the spear back?" He felt a sigh of relief. "I assume that we can be released as soon as possible so that I can complete my transaction?"

"I'm afraid that won't be possible," he said. "Because the spear originated in Jerusalem, it is the property of the Israeli government. We thank you for returning it to its rightful owners."

Django jumped to his feet. "That's ridiculous. The spear hasn't been in this land for two thousand years. It's passed through more historical hands than a Roman coin, and I acquired it fair and square. I own it, not a country that didn't exist when Jesus was crucified."

"Sit down, now." He pointed to the chair. "This is not debatable. Israelites occupied this land a thousand years before the Christian era. The state owns any of the artifacts found or established here, and I am its chosen emissary. The decision is final."

Django seethed. There was no way he could let this stand, not after the thousands of miles and many lives he'd put at risk.

"Then, I demand reparations." He pounded the table. "Your religion was founded on justice, and you owe me what I would have received from Mohammed."

Zamir stood and walked to the single barred window, and stared out into the desert light. "You have no idea about our religion, philosophy, or way of life. It's irrelevant what you think. You'll just be fortunate if you ever see your homeland again."

"Bullshit." The veins in his neck tightened. "I was born a wandering Jew. I understand the need to protect your homeland. I get it that all a man really has is his mind and the condition of his heart. And I know that Judaic law is the basis for western law and ethics. You know you have to compensate me."

Zamir put his hands on the table, leaned across it and stared into Django's eyes. "You gave up being a Jew decades ago in your pursuit of your selfish goals. You will never understand our divine mandate to protect and expand our God-given territory. We will do whatever we have to do to preserve our goals."

Anahita stood. "You don't believe in the God of Abraham," she yelled. "You're nothing but a Zionist, and this is exactly why there will never be peace between you and us."

"And who is it that you represent?" He walked around

the table and stood over her. "You come from a dictatorship bent on our destruction. Do you not think that your madmen leaders would readily push a button to annihilate us?"

"Perhaps. I don't know about that," she said. "I don't like them either. But, until the West recognizes Palestine and its right to Jerusalem, there will never be lasting peace with the other Arab states."

"They will never have Jerusalem. That is our solemn oath."

"East Jerusalem will be the capital city of Palestine." She glared into his eyes. "And the Temple Mount will always belong to Islam."

You are a hypocrite," he shouted. "While you think you stand for freedom and justice, you are a citizen of a demonic Islamic regime that kills its own people."

"I am not my government."

"Well, I am," he said.

"Are you aware of Mohammed's intentions with the spear?" Django asked. "He's a player in this brewing battle for Jerusalem."

"I am fully aware."

A soldier stuck his face in the door. "Sir, our intelligence has just informed us that the enemy is deploying some Scud rockets."

"Thank you," Zamir said, and then turned back to

Django. "I'll deal with you later. But I will be watching your every move."

"Why don't you do something to stop the Raptor? He was just here somewhere."

"Did it occur to you that we might be allies?" Zamir glanced to the wall on his right. "We have him and your friends in custody in the next room."

"What?" he said. "Well, don't give him access to my spear."

"As a matter of fact." He strode toward the door. "He has both of the relics, even as we speak."

Zamir exited. Two armed guards hustled in behind him. Within seconds, another soldier entered followed by Ghost, Celeste, Lydia, the Raptor, and then another armed guard. Django wanted to comfort Celeste, but a sentry blocked him.

The Raptor sat in the chair Zamir had vacated. "Sit down." He motioned to Django. "We're going to settle this once and for all."

A deafening explosion rocked the room, driving everyone to the floor. As dust and debris choked the air, Django crawled slowly through the smoke toward Celeste's screams.

Chapter 22
Checkpoint

Django felt like he was hacking up a lung. As he crawled through the debris, his head pounded from the explosion. Broken glass tore at his hands and knees. The ceiling had fallen in on top of them. Celeste's screams had turned into moans of pain.

A soft glow emanated from a spot on the littered floor. Suspended dust particles danced in the light, forming a double oval that looked like a magnetic field. Then, the shaft of light morphed into a DNA twisted ladder and climbed into the desert sky. He shook his head. Was this for real?

Reaching through the spinning vortex toward the radiance on the floor, he found the handle of a spear lying across the ceiling tiles. He grabbed it with his left hand, and continued to crawl. Blood from the knee wound oozed down his exposed leg. He fought against the encroaching darkness in his head.

When he reached Celeste he found part of the ceiling had landed across her stomach. He struggled to his feet in order to get more leverage on the interlaced two-by-fours. When he stood, he was grabbed around his own legs in a football tackle that brought him crashing back down onto the rubble.

He raised his head. At his feet kneeled the Raptor, staring at him with his one good eye. Blood dripped under the patch on his other eye.

"Give me my spear." The Raptor yelled as he raised the other spear above his head.

Then, he swung it down wildly. Django quickly spread his legs as the blade narrowly missed his crotch and smashed against the ceiling tiles on the floor.

Django leaped to his feet. "The spear is not yours."

The Raptor, now also on his feet, slashed at Django's head. He blocked the blade with his spear. The madman slashed at his stomach. He folded like a jackknife as the blade missed by inches. Then, someone grabbed his arms and handcuffed them behind him.

He craned his head to see who had restrained him.

"You got the wrong guy," he said. "That maniac over there attacked me."

The Israeli soldier forced Django to the ground, as

another soldier grabbed the Raptor. A third man in uniform pulled the framing from Celeste's abdomen. Then he kneeled to examine her.

"All three of you have serious injuries and you will all be escorted to the Hadassah Medical Center."

Django tried to snake himself toward Celeste. "Is she going to be all right?"

"She's breathing," said the soldier.

He and two ambulance attendants lifted Celeste onto a gurney. One medic held a bag with a tube and an IV dripping into Celeste's arm.

"Where are Ghost and Anahita?" he asked.

"Your friends are already in an ambulance headed for the hospital."

"Are they both okay?"

The soldier picked him up and then nudged him toward the door. "Cuts and bruises, but beyond that, I can't say for sure."

"What about Lydia?" The Raptor asked the soldier.

"The lady in black? She was unconscious, but breathing."

"Take me to her, immediately" he demanded. "And remove my handcuffs. I am a personal friend of your commander."

"I understand that," the soldier said. "But, it's also my

duty to prevent any violence."

"You have my word," said the Raptor.

"Mine, too." Django wasn't going to let him gain any advantage.

They walked side by side in front of the soldier and out of the demolished building. He felt encased by the sweltering sand. Sweat poured down his face as he approached the ambulance.

Celeste lay on the left lower bunk. Two medics hovered over her. Django lifted himself up on the bunk above her. The Raptor squeezed into the upper berth across from him. The soldier slammed the doors shut, and then sat on the lower bunk opposite Celeste. He nestled his automatic rifle in his lap in the ready position.

"Let's get out of here," he yelled to the driver as he banged on the wall of the military ambulance.

Django tried to lie down, but the pain in his head and the threat from the Raptor kept him awake for the ride.

"Where are my spears?" he asked the soldier.

The man just stared ahead.

"Are they on this ambulance?" The Raptor asked.

The soldier hesitated. "Yes."

Django goosed his neck around the head of the standing medic and peered at the Raptor. "Those are still my relics. You have no claim to them."

"Roth," he said. "You have no idea what you've walked into, do you?"

Django reached down, found Celeste's hand, and squeezed it softly. "I know that we had a deal for you to buy the spear, and I'm holding you to it."

"The deal is null and void because you tried to trick me."

"You would have received the real spear when we came to terms and made the actual exchange."

"When the new world manifests, you won't need your precious spear or any money," he said. "Because the foretold Kingdom will be at hand."

Celeste groaned. The medic placed an oxygen mask over her face and hung the IV bag from the ambulance ceiling just above Django's head.

"What do you know about kingdoms, other than your own hellish prison-world?" He glared at the Raptor. "If there is a God, He wouldn't have anything to do with a cold blooded killer like you."

"Judge not, young man," he said. "The so-called righteous have always killed their heathen enemies, and vice versa. The God of Abraham and the Angel of Darkness will sort out their tribes. We each have a role in this eternal drama, whether we acknowledge it or not."

"I'm not exactly sure what you have planned for the

Temple Mount," he said. "But I'm sure it won't benefit anyone except you."

"On the contrary, my bestowal will save mankind from the endless warfare that is centered on this sacred ground, although it may be painful in the short term." He leaned forward to look out the front window. "You're the selfish one who wants my money in order to live a life of myopic luxury."

"You don't know anything about me." Django swallowed back the bile in his throat. "Did it ever occur to you that I might want the money for another reason?"

"Like what?" He chuckled. "An island like mine off the coast of Belize?"

"No," he answered. "Although it's none of your business, a home with care for my father."

Celeste groaned and shifted. He looked down at her and the medics checking her vital signs.

"Is she okay?" he asked.

"She appears to have sustained internal injuries," the medic said. "Don't worry, she'll get the best trauma care in the world from the experts at the medical center."

Barbed wire and a guard tower appeared on the right hand side of the road. He spotted some graffiti art, one of a girl clutching a balloon that was sailing over the barrier separating the Palestinians from the Jews. They approached the Qalandia checkpoint. He hoped they wouldn't stop him from entering West Jerusalem.

The ambulance driver switched on his siren to get through the border cluster. An Israeli guard at the checkpoint looked in the window and then waved them through.

The Raptor gave the thumbs up to the guard and then looked at Django. "So you care for someone other than yourself?"

"What a brilliant observation." He realized he was clutching her hand too tightly. "What did you suppose this was all about?"

"I thought like most of your activities, she was a relationship born of convenience."

"You know," he said. "The world would be a better place if you weren't in it."

"Touché." The Raptor wiped away a stream of blood seeping under his eye patch. "You may get a portion of your wish soon enough."

They passed within eyesight of the Mount Moriah. On its top, the golden Dome of the Rock gleamed in the sunlight like an icon jewel. When they arrived at the Hadassah Medical Center, orderlies were waiting to unload the patients. They reached for Django, but he shook his head and pointed to Celeste.

"Take her first," he said. "Please treat her gently."

After they transported Celeste into the facility, Django and the Raptor were placed on gurneys and wheeled into the emergency foyer that smelled of antiseptic and teemed with people needing attention.

"Is this normal?" Django asked the attendant.

"The hostilities have started," the man said. "They're shelling villages north of us even as we speak.

The Raptor clasped his hands and smiled. "All according to plan." Then, he summoned an administrator and whispered something in his ear.

Django winced as he lifted his injured leg and bloodstained shoe onto the footstep of the wheelchair. "You are one demented son of a bitch."

An IDF soldier appeared and wheeled the Raptor toward a pair of swinging doors. He turned and looked back over his shoulder at Django.

"I'm sure I'll see you tomorrow morning at the Golden Gate?" he asked. "You wouldn't want to miss being at the epicenter of the advent of the Millennial Age, now would you?"

"Where are my spears?" he yelled back at him and to anyone who might listen.

The doors swung shut behind the wheelchair. Amid the cacophony of tongues and the cries of the injured, his solitary voice was drowned.

Chapter 23

Awakening

"Mr. Roth? Mr. Roth? Is there a Mr. Roth in the waiting room?"

"Huh? What?" He must have been in daze thinking about the swirl of events over the last few days. He tried to raise his hand, but a zip tie bound his hands.

"He's right here," said a voice.

He turned to see an Israeli guard standing just behind him and pointing him out.

The nurse nodded, then disappeared through the door. A doctor came out, walked over, and sat beside him.

"Sir," he said. "Celeste may be in danger of losing her baby."

"Her baby? What baby? How is she? Can I see her?"

"You didn't know she was pregnant?" The doctor looked concerned. "She indicated you were the father."

"Wow. I had no idea." *My God, I might be a father.* "I

have to see her. What's her condition?"

"Easy, Mr. Roth, one thing at a time. I can see this may be a bit of a shock."

"*May* be?"

The doctor's pager buzzed, and he scanned the message.

"I have an emergency," he said. "We'll be getting a lot more of these as this war heats up." He rose from his seat. "She'll have to stay here for a couple of days. The next twenty-four to thirty-six hours will tell the tale."

"Wait a minute." He grabbed the doctor's sleeve. "What tale? Is her life in danger too?"

"Frankly, sir, it could be. It depends if there are further complications from the pregnancy." He shook Django's hand. "We just need to keep her calm and under close observation."

"Please, I must see her." He looked at the doctor, then up at the guard who frowned and shook his head. "You can't turn me down. Imagine if it were your wife."

The doctor whispered something in the soldier's ear.

"Very well, but this is against my better judgment." The doctor summoned a nurse, then turned back to him "You cannot do anything to agitate her. Do you understand?"

"Of course I do."

The nurse wheeled Django into a room and then

stopped the wheelchair next to Celeste's bed. Then she turned and opened the curtains around the adjoining bed.

The soldier took a position by the door. "Don't forget what the doctor said."

"Do I look like I have a memory problem?"

Django raised himself out of the chair. He leaned over, moved aside the oxygen tube in Celeste's nostrils, and kissed her on the lips. She stirred, but didn't wake up.

"She's been like that since right after they gave her the pain medication."

Surprised, he whipped around. "Anahita. I've been wondering about you?"

She rose up on her elbows, then threw her legs over the side of her bed and sat up.

"I've been better," she said. "I'm still a little woozy, but I'll live. How are you?"

"Same thing. My leg is killin' me, but at least they stopped the bleeding." He thumped his knee. "At least I can walk."

"What's with him?" She thumbed at the guard.

"I guess I'm a security risk."

"I'm not deaf," said the soldier. "And you are a national risk."

Django and Anahita exchanged glances

"I want to talk to someone from the American

embassy?" he said.

The soldier shook his head.

"I want asylum in the United States," she said.

For the first time, the soldier looked puzzled.

"I know you have diplomatic relations with the USA," she said. "And they are your allies in this war. I demand to speak to a representative."

The soldier keyed the microphone on his shoulder and stepped out of the room.

Django took a bite of Anahita's ice cream. "I didn't know you were going to do that."

"Neither did I until right now, but it makes sense."

"Where's Ghost?" he asked.

"I don't know." She glanced at the door. "When we were all in triage, the Raptor came in with some soldiers. They grabbed Lydia and Ghost and hurried away."

"How was Ghost?"

"He had a few lacerations, but he appeared to be okay."

"What about Lydia?"

"Her arm was in a splint, and she was in pain, but she was semi-alert."

Django searched through the medical cabinet, found a pair of scissors and gave them to her. She cut loose his hands, then hacked off the long leg of his pants.

"Might as well look like an international spy."

"Or a porn actor." He looked down at his outfit. "The black shorts, black socks and black leather shoes speak volumes. Did anyone say anything about the spears?"

"The Raptor had one of them in his hand."

The soldier opened the door, then held it open for a gray-haired man in a designer suit that carried a briefcase. Django quickly shoved the scissors in his slack's pocket. The soldier pulled out a pair of handcuffs and headed quickly toward Django.

The man stood in front of the advancing soldier. "Wait."

The soldier pulled his revolver. "We should have eliminated him when we had the chance."

"Stand down," the suited man said.

The soldier backed against the wall, but kept his .45 at his side.

The suit stuck out his hand. "Hello," he said. "I'm Jacob Stein, assistant to the American ambassador." He shook each of their hands. "I know who both of you are. How can I be of assistance?"

"You can get me and my friends the bloody hell out of here."

"Anything else?"

"I want my spears back."

"I'm sorry," he said. "We don't have your relics. We

thought you might be able to tell us where they are."

The guard sneered.

"What's this all about?" Django searched his face. "How is it that my own back-stabbing government that has an international conflagration brewing cares so much about me and my business?"

Stein placed his briefcase on the medical cart, and then pulled out an eight-and-a-half by eleven-inch photograph and handed it to him.

"Do you recognize that moment?" he asked.

Django threw the picture back on the tray and it slid off and onto the floor.

"Do you think I'm stupid?" He gritted his back teeth. "That's a picture of the twin towers just after the 9/11 bombings. What's that act of terrorism got to do with what we're discussing?"

Stein handed the photograph to the soldier who ground it under his boot. He turned back to Django. "Nothing is as it seems, Mr. Roth. Perhaps we can make a trade."

Chapter 24
Revelation

Like feuding conjoined twins, confusion and pain competed for his logical thoughts. He had to get out of the hospital and find his friends before the Raptor got his hooks in him again. Maybe he should be asking himself who were his real friends? Now he had his own government throwing him a monkey wrench.

"What's the point of showing me a photo of the destruction of the World Trade Center Towers?" Django asked. "All I want to know is can you get us out of here?"

"You had a visceral reaction to that memory, did you not?" asked Stein.

"Of course," he answered. "Like everyone else I was sick and horrified."

"And in a very short space of time, the government told you who to hate for the crime, right?"

Django felt the familiar knot in his belly. "Well, we all

knew it was Al-Qaeda. So?"

"Did we?" Stein raised his eyebrows. "The American public never heard of Al Qaeda until the president named that group after the attacks."

"Okay, so what?"

"Follow the real beneficiaries. However, it's not important that you know who or what caused that calamity. It was an entirely logical outcome of advanced planning and social engineering. We control so-called reality by manipulating mass consciousness through the organs of communication."

"So you think you control my mind?"

"Not per se," he said. "We merely influence the reality construct within which you think and act."

"You're nuts," Django said. "My reality is separate from yours and I want to get out of this madness."

"Come with me." Stein opened the door and motioned for the guard to stay "I want to show you something."

"I'm coming too." Anahita said.

"You might as well. You're in this too."

They walked down a tiled corridor and entered a room that looked like a small lecture hall, with a silver screen hanging behind a lectern, and a LCD projector dangling from the ceiling.

"Please, sit down," he said.

They sat in the theater seats. Stein dimmed the lights and brought up a genealogy chart that looked like a tree with two main branches and one common root. One offshoot traced the lineage of Jesus Christ and the other of Mohammed, back to King David down through Abraham and eventually back to Adam at the bottom of the tree.

Django shook his head. "I'm not interested in bloodlines."

"You should be," he said. "You do understand the geopolitical heart of this impending conflict, I assume?"

"Well," he said. "No doubt it's the age-old dispute between Israel and the Palestinians about who owns Jerusalem. But what does that have to do with me?"

"Or me?" Anahita chimed in. "I'm Iranian. Other than the Palestinians getting forever screwed by the Zionists, I don't really care about the conflict."

"We need your help," said Stein. "Your countries need your help."

"You need my help?" he asked. "I'm just a businessman who's trying to reclaim his property and get back home."

Stein flipped on the lights. "And that's all any of these people want. Except, what is essentially a local conflict between neighbors over about 35 acres of land is about to turn into an international conflagration."

Django squinted. "And what am I supposed to do about that?"

"For starters, you have the Spear of Destiny, and second, you are an heir of the Davidic bloodline."

"I *had* the spear," he said. "And I've never been informed that I'm related to King David."

"We have traced your Roth lineage back to the house of David. He turned to Anahita. "You should understand that. Mohammed, peace be unto his name, was also a descendant of David."

"You don't need the phony sanctity." She glared at him. "I know that."

Django glanced at her, then back at Stein. "Well, that's interesting, but I'm not devout. Why do you care about me when I'm not necessarily religious-minded?"

"I want you to meet a colleague who is more familiar with these elements."

Stein opened the adjoining wood and glass paneled door. A bearded man wearing suspenders and Ben Franklin spectacles walked into the room.

"This is Dr. Mikael Diamond, Director of Metaphysics, U.S. Department of Defense." Stein bowed and departed.

Django extended his hand. "I didn't know the United States had a Department of Metaphysics."

"Hardly anyone does," he replied. "It was secretly

created in early 1943 when the War Department had to counter the Nazi preoccupation with supernatural power."

"Then, can you conjure up the magic to find my spear and get us the hell out of here before this whole region turns into a glass parking lot?"

"That's not my mission," he said. "I'm here to make an attempt to answer any questions you might have about your role in this conflict."

Django coughed. "My role? What role? All I know is that this Stein dude says I'm related to King David. Now, how the hell does that compute? How do you know about me and that I was going to end up in Israel?

"Part luck, part planning," he said. "We've been tracking you for a long time. It's our job to keep track of people who are connected to the Davidic bloodline and have, uh, relics."

"Then you knew of the spear too?" Django asked.

"Of course," he said. "The person you got it from stole it from us."

"Us, meaning the United States?" he asked. "How did you get it?"

"We've had it since General Patton liberated it in Berlin in the closing days of the war in Europe."

"And how am I involved in all this?" Anahita asked.

"The agency has been active with the counter-revolutionary forces in Iran since the revolution in '79," he said. "You remember the call you received telling you to go to the Internet Café and be on the lookout for an American?"

"Yes," she said. "But it was from one of my friends in the movement."

Diamond just smiled.

"So, you arranged for all this?" Django was burning. "You knew all this shit was going to go down, and you didn't intervene? You owe her and me an apology. And you need to compensate me for the spear that I traded for in good faith, fair and square."

"That's within the realm of reason," Diamond said. "However, you need to understand that we've lost the man you call the Raptor, Ghost and the spear. And – I hate to admit this - they may be right under our noses. That's why we need your help. You help us and we'll get you home. No one else can help you."

"And the spear?"

"We'll have to talk about that," Diamond said. "First we have to locate the spear."

"I don't have it."

"We need it by tomorrow night on the Foundation Stone."

"Are you going to help me get out of here, or are you

just jackin' me around like everyone else?"

"I am not jackin' you around, as you say," he said. "I can see you're not informed."

"Of the Foundation Stone? I've heard of it. Isn't it somewhere on the Temple Mount?"

Anahita frowned. "That's the occupier's name. We call it Haram-al-Sharif or the Noble Sanctuary."

"You're both right," he said. "The Foundation Stone is the central geologic formation within the main iconic structure of Old Jerusalem, the Dome of the Rock."

"This is what they are fighting over?" Django scratched his head. "A rock?"

"More than just any rock," he said. "The Jews believe it is the very intersection of heaven and earth, from which Yahweh created the world. Abraham was willing to sacrifice his son on this rock. It was also the central location of both of the Jewish Temples, where the Holy of Holies stood - where the Arc of the Covenant sat."

"That's blasphemy," Anahita said. "We do know that Mohammed ascended to heaven on his night journey from this holy location."

"Point well taken." The doctor nodded. "I'm just trying to reconcile these differences. We're your friends."

"You're not telling me what I want to hear," Django said.

"Well," he said. "I'm sorry about that. You know you're implicated in a number of international crimes."

"Circumstantial."

"Maybe. Maybe not. But you better listen if you want our help."

Django nodded. He knew he was momentarily trapped.

"That's a little better," Diamond said. "My point is that this spot has existed as a vortex point for all three of these Abrahamic faiths since each of their inceptions."

"Okay, I can buy that." Django narrowed his eyes. "But who owns it? I thought the Israeli's control it."

"Yes and no. Israeli General Moshe Dayan turned the management of the site over to the Waqf, a Muslim council, after Israel captured the Old City in the '67 war."

"Why would he do that?" Django asked. "The Israeli's could have kicked the Muslims off the mount and avoided more than forty years of war."

"As a gesture of peace."

"Didn't work very well, did it?" He stood. "Okay, so why me?"

Diamond took off his glasses and wiped them with his handkerchief. "We want you to help us return the mount to the world."

"Without causing World War III? That's impossible."

"We believe you with possession of the spear can

change that."

"Sounds like science fiction." He rubbed his chin.

"Believe me, it is not, and we are your only protection."

"You know," he said. "I can't do anything without finding the spear, and to do that you must leave me completely alone. You can't track me."

"Without the spear you are worthless to us."

"I need time."

Diamond looked at his watch." You have twelve hours."

"I might need more."

The director shook his head. "At midnight we pull the trigger whether you're with us or not."

"You better hope I find the spear and it changes the negative outcome you envision."

"We can only hope the metaphysical component works," he said. "Our colleagues can control the physical manifestations of reality and its consequences, but we're not yet well-versed in the metaphysical components that underlie that collectively agreed upon reality."

Django exhaled deeply. "Well, shit," he said.

Chapter 25
Symbol in the Desert Sand

Ghost picked the spear up off the table and ran his thumb across the blade. His head still throbbed from the explosion and he wasn't quite sure how long he'd been in the ramshackle house of a Bedouin tribesman. He needed to find Django.

He remembered that a driver had picked up the Raptor, Lydia and him in an SUV and then drove south out of Jerusalem into the endless Negev Desert. Now he sat across from the Raptor who worked on a laptop.

"Don't even think about it," the Raptor said. "You're miles from nowhere and none of these people will help you."

"What do you want from me?"

The Raptor picked up the spear. "I want you to show me how to conjure up the magic that is inherent in this relic."

"Well, we told you that it took the male and female polarities," he said. "And you know Celeste is in the hospital in Jerusalem. So, you'll just have to do it on your own."

"You'll partner with Lydia."

"I don't think so." Because there was no incantation, he had to talk his way out of any so-called ceremony. "Besides, she's injured."

The Raptor typed something on his computer, waited a beat, then typed again.

"She'll be here in a minute or two, and we can get started."

A trickle of sweat dripped underneath his arm, but no way was he going to let this madman know about his nervousness.

Ghost stood. "You mind if I step outside and use my cell?"

The Raptor blocked his way, and then grabbed the cell out of his hands. "You can't do that. I'm not ready to announce where we are through the tracking of your cell phone."

"I thought your money protected you everywhere you went."

"I have friends and enemies in every region," he said. "And that includes the government of Israel."

"I need to find my friend."

"You need to summon the magic for me."

"How is it that you can work on that computer and not worry about them finding you?"

"They know where I am," he said, "Besides, we use an encryption program in Bedouin Arabic. They skipped the industrial age altogether. Went straight to the digital age and off the grid."

He sure wished he could get his phone back or his hands on that computer.

"I still don't understand what you're going to do with the spear."

"Simple," he said. "Take the temple back for the Master. If it takes a war for the people to accept that leadership, then so be it."

"And the spear is going to help by doing what?" His words were cut off by Lydia, who was being wheeled through the door by a Bedouin attendant. She had gauze wrapped around her head. The Raptor jumped up to hug his daughter.

"How are you feeling," he asked her.

"I've been better," she said. "Let's get this ceremony started so I can get back and lie down."

The Raptor took the other spear out of a large briefcase and laid it on the table next to the one Ghost had been handling.

"I don't know which one is real," he said. "I expect your ritual to divulge that."

Ghost picked up the other one. "And if it doesn't?"

"I guess we won't need you any more."

The Bedouin pulled back his cloak to reveal an Uzi machine gun.

Ghost swallowed hard. "Well, all right then. Let's get this party started.

He searched his memory for something that might work. There was nothing in his Garifuna upbringing that he could draw on. *Think.* Symbols. There was something from his metaphysical studies.

They walked out into the blistering Negev sun. The Bedouin climbed into the SUV and started the engine. Ghost took the two spears from the Raptor and kneeled on the ground. With one of them he began to scratch in the sand. He drew a number seven, then at the bottom of the numeral he began a circle from the six o'clock position, going counter clockwise. When he got to the nine o'clock position, he drew toward the middle of the circle. At the intersection with the leg of the seven that bisected the semi-circle, he scratched an infinity sign. Then, he took one spear and stabbed it into the middle of the right loop in the infinity, and then buried the other spear in the left loop.

"Now what?" The Raptor paced.

"I need your silence," he said. "And your concentration. Both of you sit like me, in the lotus position, around the spears."

The Raptor struggled to fold his legs. Lydia, although she appeared to have a head wound and a concussion, assumed the classic position as if it were natural for her.

"I want both of you to say the Om sound with me," he said. "Close your eyes. Start the sound in your belly and move it up your core and finish in your head."

"I've done this before," the Raptor said.

Ghost glanced at the Bedouin who had gotten out of the car.

"Aauuummmm," Ghost chanted. "May the holy spirit return to the lance."

The Raptor and Lydia aumed and chanted with him.

He glanced again at the Bedouin. As he did he noticed a slightly perceptible shiver emanate from the spear in the right orb of the infinity.

"Make our triangle tighter," he said to them. "We need to hold hands now."

The Raptor frowned, but grabbed his hand, and then reached out with his other one to hold Lydia's. Their circle/triangle was complete.

"Aauuummmm." They chanted in unison again.

"I invite the spirit of Allah to empower the sword."

The Bedouin moved closer to observe. The spear emitted a low humming sound.

"Aauuummmm. I invite Yahweh to manifest in the lance that lies before us."

The Bedouin was practically standing over them. He was sure the spear was beginning to glow and that only he was noticing the subtle changes.

The Raptor stared, looking enraptured by the experience. "How much longer?"

Ghost grabbed the vibrating spear, and then quickly put Lydia in a chokehold, and stood her up. "It's done."

The Bedouin raised his Uzi, but the Raptor put his arm in front of him.

"Leave her alone," he said. "And I'll see that you have safe passage out of the desert."

"Just like the chance you give everyone else? I don't think so." He looked at the Bedouin. "Tell him to drop his weapon in the sand."

"Do it," the Raptor said. Then he turned back to Ghost. "You won't survive this."

Ghost shuffled Lydia toward the Uzi, and then he picked it up.

"Then neither will she."

"Don't worry darling," he said to Lydia. "I won't let

anything happen to you."

"I can take care of myself," she said.

Ghost backed her toward the idling SUV. He pushed her in the driver's seat, pointed the Uzi at her and then turned back toward the two men.

"Thanks for cooling off the interior," he said. "Black absorbs so much heat."

With the Bedouin running after him in his rear view mirror, he screamed into the dust of the Negev Desert.

Chapter 26

Murder in the Hospital

Django had until midnight to find the spear. Diamond had loaned him an unmarked Renault electric car, but Ahmed, the guard in the passenger seat, was the wrong end of the bargain. He glanced in his rear view mirror at Anahita in the back seat who seemed to be writing text messages. Now, he just needed to gather the spear, Celeste and Ghost and get out of Dodge before the wheels fell off.

After he stopped at a red light, he pulled the cell phone out of his jacket pocket and hit the numbers.

"It's illegal in Israel to talk on the cell while you're driving," Ahmed said.

"Arrest me."

"I might do more than that if you're not careful."

"Ghost, is that you?" Django couldn't believe he'd finally reached him on the sat phone. "Where are you?"

"Yeah it's me. I'm somewhere in the Negev," Ghost

replied. "I just got away from the Raptor, and I have Lydia with me in a SUV."

"Where's the spear?"

"I have it with me."

"The authentic one?"

"I think so," Ghost said. "If my intuitive powers are still intact."

"Great, we have to meet up somewhere and figure out a way to get out of Israel."

"Absolutely," Ghost said. "Where do we meet?"

Django glanced at Ahmed who stared out the window.

"How about at the hospital? " he said. "We have to get Celeste."

"Okay," Ghost said. "I can be there in about an hour."

"See you then." Django snapped the phone shut and put it back in his pocket.

"You know you're not leaving Jerusalem until you deliver the spear to Diamond on the Temple Mount," Ahmed said.

He clenched his teeth. "Oh yeah, that little detail. I need some Muslim clothes or we may have to skip that part."

Ahmed patted the bulge in his left breast pocket. "I don't think so."

Django parked the car in the hospital lot and ran toward the entrance. Ahmed followed close behind.

"I'll catch up to you later," Anahita yelled to him.

Without turning around, Django waved back at her, then hustled in the door, past the guards, past the elevator, up the stairs and finally into Celeste's room. A trail of hospital security followed him like a pack of dogs. Only the flash of Ahmed's Mossad badge stopped them from cuffing and hauling him away.

The attendant, who looked like Nurse Ratched, put up both of her hands. "This is not visiting hours," she said. "You all have to leave. Now."

The pursuing posse grumbled, but turned around and shuffled out. Django stood over Celeste with Ahmed pulling at his jacket.

"How is she?" he asked.

"She's resting a little more comfortably now," the nurse said. "But, you will still have to leave."

Ahmed began jerking him out of the room. Django pulled away.

"How's the baby?" His heart raced.

The nurse tried to restrain him. "You'll need to talk to the doctor."

"I don't have time," he said. "Time is running out for all of us."

Ahmed cuffed him and dragged him out the door.

"Go to the waiting room," she said. "I'll send the doctor

as soon as he is available. I can assure you that she will be okay."

With Ahmed pushing him toward the elevator he stumbled against the tiled floor.

"Stop shoving me and take these handcuffs off," he demanded. "I can't get the damned spear unless my hands are free. Ghost will spot a rat in a heartbeat."

"If I do, you better act civilized or I'll cuff you again and smack you upside the head, I swear."

"No problem," he said. "I just had to know. You'd be the same with your family."

When they got to the lobby, Ghost was waiting. He had his hands on the back of a wheelchair into which Lydia was strapped. He looked like he'd stolen and donned some hospital scrubs. Lydia yelled for help.

Ghost waved off people who approached and just kept repeating, "Mental patient. Mental patient."

Django gave Ghost a hug and smiled at Lydia.

"Nice touch," he said. "But, we can't have her screaming like this."

"Yeah, really," Ghost said. "I was going to knock her out, but I still have an issue about hitting a woman. Even her."

"You hit me," Lydia said. "And I swear I'll kill you."

Ahmed flashed his badge and whispered to a security

guard who ushered the group into an empty operating room.

The OR suite was cool like a meat locker. It smelled like antiseptic. A single gurney, bathed under a floodlight, sat in the middle of the room.

"You better make this quick," Ahmed said to Django. "I don't like the feel of this."

"Okay, where's the spear?" Django asked Ghost.

Ghost took off his scrub pants to reveal shorts and the spear strapped to his bare leg.

Django grabbed the relic and put it on the gurney under the bright light. He found a scalpel nearby and scraped at the butt of the spear. He got frustrated and scraped deeper.

"What are you looking for?" Ghost asked.

"The microchip imbedded in the base."

"Who put it there?"

Django grabbed another pick-like instrument. "Whoever had it before me and wanted to track it."

Ahmed stepped closer to the table. "What is this thing?"

"Some say the past, the present and the future." He threw the spear on the ground. "But this sure ain't it."

"I must have grabbed the wrong one." Ghost rubbed his forehead.

Ahmad kneeled over the spear. He looked up at Django. "Then, it looks like we have no more business together."

As he reached into his breast pocket, he was bowled

over by a company of green clad troopers. A soldier quickly escorted Ahmed out of the room. Another man plunged a hypodermic syringe into Ghost's neck. He collapsed on the floor.

The Raptor walked through the door and untied Lydia from her wheelchair. Then, he hugged her. "Are you ok, my love?"

She gave him a slight smile, then kicked Ghost in the balls, but he was too gone too respond.

"Strap him to the gurney," the Raptor said, and pointed to Django.

Two more soldiers wheeled Celeste into the room, and rolled her up to his left side. She was wide-eyed and strapped to her hospital bed.

"You can't do this," Django said. "I'm protected by the Mossad."

"The Mossad works for me." He walked over to the television and turned it on. "As the three of you die together, you can watch the final victory unfold."

The Raptor stuck the needle in Celeste's neck and then did the same to Django. Then, a guard wheeled Ahmad into the room and to the right side of Django's gurney. Then, all of the other soldiers left, and took Lydia with them.

Ahmed tried to say something, but he had obviously been drugged to the verge of unconsciousness. The Raptor pulled out a pistol with a silencer on it, walked up to Ahmed, and shot him once in the temple, killing him instantly. He wiped the gun with his handkerchief, and then walked over to Django, unstrapped his hands and feet, and put the gun in his hand.

"Nice shot, deadeye." The Raptor laughed.

Django could barely focus on anything. The announcer on the television droned on and on about people taking shelter. He saw the form of the Raptor exit out the door. The clicking shut of locks was the last thing he remembered before it all faded to black.

Chapter 27
Lev Bernal

Was it a cave? No, it was more like a tunnel. Celeste's face floated above the bright opening. He was being drawn to the radiance like steel to a magnet. A sense of peace – something he hadn't felt in a long time – engulfed his consciousness.

"Django." A detached voice beckoned.

Leave me alone. I'm ready to go.

"Django." The voice was more insistent. The light faded.

He felt his essence collapse back into his head and chest.

"Django, wake up."

He struggled to open his eyes. The pain in his head suggested he was alive – but barely.

"Can you give him another shot?" A woman's voice echoed through the room.

Through his blurred vision he made out a man in a white coat, maybe a nurse and Anahita.

"Wha – What happened?" he asked.

Anahita put her face close to his. "They tried to kill you."

"How did you find me? Us? How're Celeste and Ghost?"

"They seem to be coming around too," she said. "The antidote appears to be working."

"What time is it?" he asked.

"About six o'clock, why?"

"Is this the same day the Raptor tried to kill me?"

"Well of course," she said. "You'd be dead if it had been any longer."

He pulled the tubes out of his arm and sat up straight.

"I have to get out of here and find the Raptor."

The nurse pushed him back down. "You can't go anywhere, buster. You nearly died."

"You don't understand," he said. "If I don't get out of here and find the Raptor and that spear, all hell is going to break loose."

"Hell may break loose anyway," the nurse said and pointed toward the television set.

"A world war is just around the corner," the announcer said. Images of Israeli and American jets filled the screen

combined with shots of aircraft carriers in the
Mediterranean and the Red Sea. Opposition tanks and
infantry squatted on the Lebanese and Syrian borders.
Iranian troops gathered on the Iraqi frontier, ready to march
across Iraq.

"Could this be the beginning of the war to end all wars,
the conquering of Jerusalem, and the destruction of Israel?"
The anchorman asked his unseen audience. "The Egyptian
and Saudi governments have sided with the opposition in
spite of their now decades-long peaceful relationship with
Israel."

"Now, do you understand the gravity of letting me find
him and the spear?"

"No, I don't," the nurse said. "What could you possibly
do to change any of this? It would take an act of God to stop
this thing now. Besides, with the murder of the guard, this is
a crime scene, and you couldn't leave even if you wanted
to."

The nurse plugged back in the two IVs and then left the
room.

Django grabbed Anahita by the arm. "See if there are
any guards stationed by the door."

"What for? You heard the nurse."

"Since when do you answer to any authority?" he said.
"I have to get out of here. You know I couldn't possibly

have shot that guard."

"You know that and I know that, but these Zionists have a different story."

She shook her head and walked toward the door.

He turned back to the television.

"Now, on another side of this developing story, we go to Lev Bernal, who is at the Hadassah Medical Center. Good evening Lev."

Anahita came back to his bedside. "There's no one out there at the moment. They're probably out eating some Palestinian for dinner."

"That's the reason all you people want to kill each other," he said. "I need someone on my side around here to help me."

"I'm not your enemy," she replied and walked back to his bedside. "You're not going to get any help from the Jews."

They both looked up at the TV set.

Images of colorful stained glass windows filled the screen.

"Inside the synagogue at the Hadassah Medical Center," Lev said. "Marc Chagall's words are just as vital now as they were in 1962 when he dedicated these beautiful works of art: 'I know that the path of our life is eternal and short, and while still in my mother's womb I learned to travel this path with love rather than with hate.' I'm going to look for some more personal stories in this hospital. I'll be back with you in a few minutes."

"We need to find that guy." Django said. "He can help me prove my innocence. We don't have much time."

"You've lost your mind." Anahita walked away.

Django pulled off the attached tubes and jumped out of bed.

Anahita groaned. "Uh, your ass is hanging out."

He looked down at his hospital gown. "When did this happen? I need some other clothes."

"I suppose they changed you between the time before you nearly died and when you woke up," she said. "I found some Muslim clothing for you."

She pulled a large paper bag out from under the hospital bed and handed him a round hat, a garment that looked like a gown, a pair of pants and sandals.

"What is this?" he asked

"It's a thoub, a kufi and an izaar," she said. "Put them on."

Still in her western clothing, she quickly disrobed and put on a burqa from the same bag.

Celeste rose up from her bed. "What the hell is going on here?"

Django walked over to her. "How are you feeling?"

"What's happening?" she asked.

He kissed her on the forehead. "Just relax," he said. "The Raptor tried to kill us by injecting a poison, but, thanks to Anahita here, the Israeli doctors saved us with the antidote. Now, I have to find someone. I'll be right back. You all stay here."

He exited the operating room and hustled over to the information desk.

"Excuse me," he said to the receptionist. "But where is the synagogue?"

"It's down that corridor." She nodded to her right. "But you can't go in there."

"It's a matter of life and death."

She looked very uncomfortable. "May I ask whose life is in jeopardy?"

He was already walking toward the synagogue. "Maybe all of ours," he said.

Chapter 28
The Plea

The hospital lobby was jammed with people. From the television news, Django knew that the shelling had intensified from the north on the Lebanese border, from the West Bank, and from Gaza in the south. Those with the most severe injuries were being transferred to the Hadassah Medical Center.

The digital clock on the wall flashed 7:30 p.m. He knew he only had until midnight to find the spear. Now, he had to find the reporter Lev Bernal who might be able to help him clear his name.

He found him as he was about to leave the building with his cameraman and producer. Django grabbed his arm.

"May I have a word with you?" he asked.

"As you can see," he said. "I'm kind of in a hurry. In case you didn't notice, we have a war going on."

He pulled away, but Django caught up to him again and

positioned himself in front of the reporter.

"What would you say if I told you I would give you an exclusive to the story of the millennium?"

Bernal's face reddened. "I'd say you were just another Islamic extremist."

"I'm not Muslim, I'm American," he said. "And I have information about a man who thinks he is the Messiah or the anti-Christ or someone who has the wherewithal to turn this conflict into a nuclear holocaust."

He hesitated, then motioned for his two companions to go on.

"Okay," he said. "You got my attention. Spill. Fast."

"Can I buy you a cup of coffee?" Django pointed toward the cafeteria. "Or more precisely, will you buy me a cup of coffee? That's a small portion of my quandary. I lost my wallet and papers somewhere between Belize and Jerusalem."

"That sounds like the perfect MO for a terrorist," he said. "What's going to keep me from turning you in to the authorities?"

"The fact that I'm innocent, my country is your staunchest ally and everything I will tell you about these circumstances is the truth."

Bernal bought two coffees and they sat at a small table in the hospital cafeteria.

"Why are you telling me these things?" he asked.

"Because I need your help," he said. "The man we're discussing, Mohammad Goldman, the Raptor, killed my Israeli guard, and tried to kill me and my friends. He's attempting to frame me in the murder, and is intent on starting World War III."

"How can one man do all that? This sounds fishy to me."

Django sipped from his coffee. "Well, for one thing, he's the richest arms dealer, if not the richest man in the world, but only a few people even know about him. He runs his empire from a well-fortified private island off the coast of Belize in the Caribbean."

"I've heard of this guy," the reporter said. "But I thought he was just another international financier. One of the big banking guys who ripped off your country."

"He is that too. He makes a lot of markets. As his daughter Lydia says, 'He's all things to all people'."

"Lydia Goldman?" he asked. "I've heard that she is the sole heir to this guy's empire."

Django removed his cap and ran his hands through his hair. "She is, and a formidable force of her own."

"So where are these people?"

"They're somewhere in Jerusalem," he said. "They kidnapped me, my girlfriend Celeste, and my friend Ghost and brought us here to take part in this crazy ritual."

"What ritual?" he asked. "Are they Satanists?"

"They could be. I don't know. But what I do know is that he has the actual Spear of Christ and plans to wreak havoc on the Temple Mount within hours."

"The Spear of Christ?" he asked. "You mean the lance the Roman soldier stuck in Jesus' side? Are you a Christian?"

"Yes, that's the one and nearly only," he said. "The one he has is the true one – which supposedly gives him the power to control the destiny of the world. And, no, I'm not a Christian. I'm sort of, uh, one of you." He cleared his throat. "My dad was a Jew."

"You're a Jew?" His mouth dropped open. "Then, what are you doing in that ridiculous Muslim outfit?"

Django took another sip and looked around the cafeteria to see if anyone was listening.

"My clothes were ripped," he said. "I have a Muslim ally in the operating room who's there with Celeste and Ghost. I want you to come with me and meet them so that you can corroborate my story."

"Just a second." Bernal grabbed his wrist. "I still don't understand why you're telling me all this. What am I supposed to do about it? There are scores of stories to cover."

"Can you operate a concealed camera?"

"Yes, we have that capability in the truck."

"Can you log video for broadcast by yourself, suitable for television with that camera?" he asked. "And can you do it alone?"

"I suppose. We've done it before. I can even broadcast live if the situation warrants." He leaned closer. "But why would I want to do that?"

"I think I could get the Raptor to spill the beans," he said. "It might clear me and expose his crazy plan to the world, and maybe stop the destruction. His ego is as large as his empire. He thinks he's on a global mission."

"I've got better things to do than chase a crazy story like this." He got up and started to leave.

Django got up with him. "Wait. Will you just come with me to the operating room for five minutes?"

"Okay," he said. "But this better be real. I've got no time for wild goose chases."

They waded through the crowd in the lobby and then entered the operating room. Ghost and Celeste were on their feet, talking. Anahita sat on the hospital bed, reading an Arabic newspaper. Over in the corner, a cop was talking to Diamond. *What the hell was he doing there?* Django had to think fast. He escorted Bernal to the center of the room.

"Everyone," he said. "This is Mr. Lev Bernal, a reporter

from local Channel 10. He thinks he can help us find the Raptor and the spear."

Bernal tried to say something, but Django interrupted him.

"And this is Mr. Mikael Diamond from the Mossad."

Diamond shook the reporter's hand then stared at Django. "You've got less than six hours to find the spear and bring it to the Dome of the Rock - Roth." He glanced at the cop. "I bought some time until midnight with the police, but after that you have no protection." Then, he left the room in a rush.

"And it was a pleasure to see you again, Mr. Diamond," Django said to the closing door. The policeman grabbed the handle and followed close on his heels.

Ghost, Celeste and Anahita gathered around Django and Bernal.

"What's going on here?" Bernal searched the faces of the group. "Is all this for real?"

"I don't know what he told you," Ghost said. "But the man doesn't lie. We're in a tough situation here."

Celeste held her stomach as she approached Bernal. "This Raptor guy stole the Spear of Christ from Django and he plans to start World War III. Is that close? That's the truth as far as we know it."

Bernal looked at Django. "Okay," he said. "What do we

need to do?"

"Celeste, you and Ghost go down to the Kidron Valley opposite the Golden Gate. He'll be there before sunrise, but we don't know precisely when. You just have to find him."

"What should I do?" Anahita asked.

"Can you find another Muslim outfit for Lev?"

"I'm pretty sure I can."

"Get it," he said. "The three of us are going to the Temple Mount."

Chapter 29
Kidron Valley

Ghost stopped walking when he was directly below the looming eastern gate to the old city. Headstones and crypts littered the hill. A full moon illuminated The Mount of Olives on his right.

"So this is the Kidron Valley." He half-said it to himself.

Celeste stumbled on the rocks as she drew near. "That's what the taxi driver said. These so-called mounts and valleys are small compared to California. The brochures also failed to mention the squalor and the charming dump site odor."

"Hey, try to stay positive, will you, please? That was earlier, this is now. We have to figure out how to find the Raptor."

"Shouldn't be too hard - if he shows at all," she replied. "There's no one else out here at this hour. I don't like the feel of this." She folded her arms below her breasts and appeared to shiver. "This is creepy."

"Let's sit down," he said.

They found a couple of jagged boulders in the dry creek bed.

Ghost carefully laid the backpack with the duplicate spear in the dirt. He rubbed his hand along the smooth edges of the rock he sat on. "You know, this could be a remnant of Solomon's Temple."

"Could be." She shook her head. "We could be the last remnants of civilization."

"Django thinks we can make a difference."

"Well, I think he's crazy," she said. "He's delusional if he thinks any of us or that spear can do anything to change the death spiral this world is in."

"We have to try." He shook the spear out of the pack and stared at it. "We just can't sit around cryin' the blues, waitin' for the world to come to an end."

She put her head in her hands. "It just seems so stupid and hopeless. I don't want to die here."

He put his arm around her shoulder. "No one wants to die." He gestured toward the Temple Mount. "I doubt that even Jesus wanted to die."

"I don't know." She choked back the tears. "He knew his destiny. I don't know mine. All I ever wanted was a family of my own."

"Did you tell Django about the baby?"

"You mean that it could be yours?" She shook her head. "There's been no time. All this has happened so fast. I just can't handle being caught between worlds."

From the direction of the Palestinian village, headlights bounced onto the creek bed.

"You suppose that's him?" she asked.

He caught his breath. "Seems like a logical conclusion, but who knows, could be Israeli troops or a Palestinian gang looking for trouble."

"I'm scared," she said.

"I can dig it." He glanced up the hill toward the Garden of Gethsemane. "What kind of shape are you in?"

"Well, there's always this pregnancy issue," she said. "But I feel okay at the moment."

"We have to move up the hill and find some cover."

He took her hand and they started to climb. They were getting out of range of the headlights, but the bright moonlight was another story.

Celeste's panting worried him. Then she stumbled and fell into the rocky slope.

"I can't make it to the top," she said.

"Okay, lay flat and try to use some of this debris for cover."

He lay prone with his head downhill, hoping that he could hear something. Celeste lay sideways behind an outcropping of cut stones.

She shrieked. "This is a friggin grave yard."

"Yeah, this is where the final judgment is supposed to take place and all these folks want to be in the first wave of being raised from the dead."

A vehicle pulled to a stop directly below them. It looked a like an oversized armored Hummer towing a horse trailer. Three armed guards piled out and began conversing.

"What the hell is that?" she said.

"Shhh," he whispered. "If I can hear them, they can hear you."

One of the guards went to the back of the trailer and unloaded a magnificent ivory-colored horse and then led the creature back to the vehicle. A figure emerged who was dressed from head to foot in white, looking like Lawrence of Arabia bathed in moon glow.

Celeste army-crawled over to Ghost and whispered directly into his ear.

"What's that all about?"

"This is freaky," he said. "All three of these warring religions have some kind of savior riding down from the Mount of Olives on a white horse to vanquish the enemies of God."

"Yeah," she whispered. "But who's God?"

"That's the big issue, isn't it?" He put his hand over her mouth. "Shhh, lets try to make out what they're saying."

"Are the rocket launchers ready?" The Raptor's voice was clearer than he expected it to be.

"They will be ready, sir, when you give the command."

"How many blasts will it take to open a hole in the Golden Gate?"

"I'm not exactly sure," the commander replied. "It could take as many as ten shots to blow all the way through that thick stone wall. But don't worry, we have sufficient ammunition and we'll complete the operation – whatever it takes."

Celeste moved her lips close to his ear again. "What is he talking about?"

Ghost put his lips to her ear. "He's going to blow a hole through the walled up Golden Gate, and then enter the Temple Mount as the conquering Messiah."

"Holy shit." she mouthed.

"I want an opening in the wall by daybreak." The Raptor's voice echoed up the canyon. "Meanwhile, I'm going to get some rest. Wake me in a couple of hours."

The Raptor crawled back inside the Hummer, followed by two of the soldiers. The remaining guard tied the steed to the bumper and set some water and hay in front of him.

Then, he went up to the machine gun turret on top of the vehicle.

Ghost looked at his watch: 11:00 p.m.

"At least we know where the Raptor is," he said.

"Yeah and he's surrounded by soldiers and armor." She rolled over. Moonlight reflected in her eyes. "What now?"

"I'm working on it," he said. "We have a little while to figure something out."

"We may have less than an hour if Django can't stall Diamond up there at the Dome of the Rock."

"I wonder where his ten thousands troops are?" He looked at her. "Did I say that out loud?"

"You most certainly did," she answered. "What ten thousand troops?"

"One of the prophecies says the Deliverer or the Dajjal - whatever you want to call him - will have one good eye, and, like the Raptor, he'll be swarthy, and ride a white horse in front of an army of ten thousand to take back the holy mountain. I think he's blended all the Abrahamic prophecies into one character who will proclaim his mantle to the world at sunrise."

"No way," she said. "You mean to tell me this crazy mofo is going to ride up here some time before dawn, and those soldier dudes down there are going to blow a hole in the wall and he's going to come galloping down like Moses, through the open gate and proclaim himself Conqueror of Jerusalem? And no one is going to stop this?"

"We are." He stood and offered his hand. Celeste got on all fours, and then stood silently with him.

"Can you make it if we go a little higher?" he whispered.

"I think so, but not very quickly."

When they got to a level spot he stopped and took out an emergency blanket from his backpack and placed it on the ground underneath an olive tree. They sat side-by-side overlooking the Old City of Jerusalem. He put his arm around her.

"You know," she said. "After the Last Supper, Jesus came up here with his disciples to pray, and then he was ratted out by Judas, and that led to his crucifixion on the next day."

"I know that story," he said. "Most scholars think they slept in a cave up there by the Church of All Nations." He pointed toward the well-lit Catholic Church with the Byzantine mosaics. "Do you believe all those myths?"

"I have to," she said. "I'm Catholic. If I don't believe the teachings, I'll be excommunicated and spend eternity in Hell."

He raised his eyebrows. "What about love-making outside the bounds of marriage? Is that a mortal sin that condemns you to the same fate?"

"Oh, Ghost." She put her head down. "Don't ask me that. I don't know anymore. All I can do is follow my heart."

She shivered and he held her close.

"I can't get warm," she said.

He picked up the flimsy blanket and replaced it with his Levi jacket.

"Lay down," he said.

She found a comfortable position on top of his jacket24 He plopped down beside her and pulled the thin wrapping over the top. It wouldn't quite cover both of them, so he put his left arm under her head and pulled Celeste closer. She snuggled against him with her left leg between his.

"Do you think we've had our last supper?" she asked.

"I couldn't testify about that," he said. "But I got a hunch the Raptor may have had his.

Chapter 30
Dome of the Rock

Django balanced himself on the narrow walkway, then leaned against the gleaming dome. Careful not to trip on his Muslim gown, he felt for the cell phone tucked in his sock. Lev Bernal duct taped the plastic satellite antenna he had smuggled in to the gold leaf covering. Even from point blank range, the gilded sheathing bathed in moonlight was spectacular. How ironic that, thanks to Anahita, they were dressed as a Muslims hiding in plain sight atop the most visible Islamic shrine in the world.

He pressed the push-to-talk feature of the Raptor's phone. "Come in Ghost."

The receiver crackled in his ear. "Django, is that you?"

"Yes it is. Where are you? Is Celeste okay?"

"Celeste is fine. We're hunkered down on the Mount of Olives, waiting for the Raptor," he answered. "Where are you?"

"We found an exit hatch in the cupola, and I'm leaning against the top of the Dome of the Rock. Lev is setting up for TV transmission."

"Where's Anahita?"

"I'm not sure. She somehow got Bernal and me past the Waqf guards and into the Dome."

"Has Diamond showed yet?" Ghost asked. "I've got 11:30. Time's running out."

Django shifted his feet. "I know. Can you get to the Raptor?"

"Not yet," he replied. "But I know where he is and what his plans are. Right now he's in an armored vehicle surrounded by guards, but I'm pretty sure he'll be riding up here on the mount sometime between now and daylight."

"Riding?"

"Yeah a white horse?"

"What the –"

"Never mind." Ghost interrupted. "I may be able to get to him when he's alone."

"Did you pick up the duplicate spear in the hospital?"

"Yes I did," he said. "I have it with me."

"I have to show something to Diamond. Can you get it to me?"

"I don't know how."

"Can you throw it up to me from the Western Wall?"

"That's a pretty long heave," he said. "What if it doesn't make it to you?"

"You got any line of any kind?"

A pause. "I've got some fishing line in my pack."

Bernal finished his installation. "We have to get out of here," he said. "We're too conspicuous." He held his watch against the transmitter. "There better be some kind of payoff for this risk."

"Hold your horses," Django said. "I have to figure out a way to get the spear up here."

"Where is it?"

"Ghost has it over on the Mount of Olives."

Bernal shook his head. "This scheme of yours is getting flakier by the minute. How about your friend, the Islamic gal?"

"She has a cell, but I don't have her number."

"Terrific." Bernal was obviously way beyond trying to hide any skepticism.

A clanking sound alerted Django to a person by the Wailing Wall who pointed toward them. He pushed the button on the cell. "Ghost, come in."

"Yeah, go ahead."

"Do you have Anahita's cell number?"

"Yes I do."

"Okay," Django said. "Call her and see if she can help

get the spear to us."

"Roger that," he responded. "What are you going to do?"

"We have to get out of here," he said. "We've been spotted."

Django and Bernal crawled back through the hatch and emerged on the catwalk inside the structure. He paused to absorb the panorama. Although the shrine was dark and vacant, moonlight bled through the upper stained glass windows and illuminated the mosaics of the cupola. In the middle of the room, The Foundation Stone gleamed like an apparition. The history that stood before him was sobering.

"Come on," Bernal said. "We can't fool around. I have some work to do."

Django's phone buzzed. He answered. "Come in Ghost."

"Anahita will have the spear, but she's outside the walls of the Temple Mount."

"Has she seen Diamond?"

"She says that right now a man is leading a group of Israeli soldiers toward the Mugrahbi Gate."

"Got to be him," he said. "Tell her to get to the head of that procession and see if it's Diamond. If it is, have her give him the spear and tell him to come alone into the Well of Souls to find me."

"We're converging now." Django could hear the stress in his voice.

"Ghost." No answer. Django checked the cell phone. It was working. He clicked it again. "Ghost, come in." Still no response.

He and Bernal were now at ground level in front of the Foundation Stone, staring at its scarred, but polished surface.

"Technically," Bernal said. "I shouldn't be here."

"You still don't think there's a big story?"

"Jury's out on that, but that's not what I'm talking about," he said. "My Rabbinate says that this is where Solomon's Temple stood. We may be standing on the spot in the Holy of Holies where the high priests, in front of the Ark of the Covenant, addressed Yahweh."

"So why can't you be here?"

"The average Jew is not purified and is unworthy to stand before God."

Django looked up at the moonlight spilling through the stained glass windows. "Boy howdy, that would be me in spades," he said. "Hopefully, the Almighty will make a special dispensation for the task at hand."

Bernal gazed down at the stone while Django observed him. His gray eyes and the chicken wire laced skin that encased them projected the countenance of a man who'd stared into the burn of a floodlight for too long. "That remains to be seen," he said.

They walked along the fence that protected the rock from the tourists. When they came to an opening, Django reached in and touched the rock.

"Smell your hand," Bernal said. "They say it's the perfume of Heaven."

He withdrew his hand and put it to his nose. It smelled of musk. In fact, the whole room seemed to fill with that scent.

A bang turned their heads to the front of the Shrine. Someone was entering.

"Where's the entrance to the Well of Souls?" Django asked.

"I've read that there's an opening on the south side of the rock."

They found the archway entrance, climbed over the chains, and then descended the stairs down into the chamber. A shaft of moonlight shone through a hole in the top of the cave. It was as if the bedrock summit of Mount Moriah was floating in space as the Muslims maintained. The floor was carpeted. When he thumped on the walls, they sounded hollow.

Bernal found a few candles and lit them, making the cave glow. Then, he kneeled on the rug and adjusted his wristwatch camera. He dialed a number on his IPhone.

"Yeah, John, this is Lev. Yeah, I'm fine. Listen, I need you to check something for me. I'm broadcasting right now from the Well of Souls under the Foundation Stone. Check the feed and see if you're getting broadcast quality audio and video."

"Great." He trained his watch on Django. "What's your name and why are we down here under the Dome of the Rock on the Temple Mount?"

He had to suppress an inappropriate chuckle. This was crazy. "My name is Django Roth. I'm from the United States and I'm here to try to stop World War III from starting."

Bernal put up his right hand and spoke into his phone in is left. "Did you get it? Okay, good. Now listen, keep your eye on the monitor. When I start broadcasting I want you to put it on the air, live. Yeah, yeah, I'll take the heat. Just do it, understand? Okay, stand by in about ten. Yeah, if this is what I think it could be, I'll take good care of you." He hung up and let out a deep sigh.

"You ready?" Django asked.

"I'm ready," he said. "Are you?"

"No other choice."

The hard heels of a man walking against the tiles echoed above them.

'It's hard to believe all the major prophets of the three religions prayed right here," Bernal said. He pointed to an indentation in the cave ceiling. "The Muslims say that's the indentation of Mohammad's head."

Django stood to feel the hollowed space. "I've read that the dead and not-yet-born souls gather down here on a regular basis."

The chains rattled above, and then footsteps reverberated on the stairs.

"Anyone down here?" Diamond's voice was clear and deep, and vibrated against cavern walls.

"Yeah, me and Lev are here."

Diamond crossed the small landing and kneeled on one knee beside the two of them.

He looked at Django and pointed to Bernal. "Who's he?"

"This is Lev Bernal. He's my assistant and friend here in Jerusalem. Lev, this is Mr. Diamond, Director of the Metaphysical Department of the United States of America."

Diamond and Bernal shook hands. "You look familiar," Diamond said.

Then he looked back at Django. "But I told you to come alone."

"Sorry, I needed his experience," he said. "And you already have the spear, don't you?"

"I have the spear, or perhaps a replica, in my briefcase, along with another device."

Django and Bernal exchanged glances. Lev turned on his broadcast watch, and folded his hands in his lap, adjusting the bezel so it pointed at Diamond.

"What else is in the case beside the spear that Anahita gave you?" Django asked him.

Diamond smiled. "Just a small nuclear apparatus."

Django and Bernal recoiled.

"Are you crazy?" Django asked.

"No," Diamond said. "Just taking charge of the chaos. And, praise be to God, you two gentlemen will be present at the creation of the New Jerusalem."

Chapter 31

Doomsday Device

An explosion jolted the entire Dome of the Rock.
Django looked up at the ceiling of the Well of Souls to see
if it was coming down. Bernal's face was ashen. Diamond
was on his cell phone.

"What the hell was that?" Django yelled.

Diamond glanced up at him. "The opening of the
Golden Gate has begun."

"You can't be serious?" Django jumped to his feet.
"You want the world to blow up?"

"I'm in control of that," he said.

"You're from the United States, for God's sake."
Django paced around the small cave. "How do you stop all
these Chinese and Arab troops from invading?"

"I have the authority."

"From whom?" he asked. "We were supposed to have a
deal that I would give you the Spear of Christ and you

would compensate me for it. Now you're blowing up the most sacred gate. You can't stop the fuse you just lit."

"One issue at a time," he replied. "First, my authority is both temporal and metaphysical. The U.S. has been given the authority by the United Nations to mediate this conflict, and I'm the official representative for the President of the United States."

"Okay, cool," Django said. "So just give me my money for the spear and we'll say 'adios'."

"You won't need the money where you're going."

"I need it for my father who can't afford the necessary medical care. I told you that already. So do you have the money so we can get the hell out of here?"

"I'm afraid I can't give you the ransom money just yet."

"Ransom money? What ransom money?"

"The money you have demanded in exchange for this nuclear weapon you've threatened to detonate."

Django was stunned. This was something entirely off the mental map he'd constructed. He glanced at Bernal who was adjusting the dial on his camera watch.

"You know that's not true," he said. "Who do you actually serve, anyway? No mortal human being would cook something like this up."

"My ultimate direction comes from the fallen angel. He

who has dominion over the earth."

Django swallowed hard. How could he process this lunacy? He thought about Ghost, Celeste and Anahita, and the child Celeste carried. He envisioned his father laying in a third-rate hospital bed, unable to get the heart surgery he needed, the millions of innocent people who were about to die.

Another explosion boomed from the direction of the eastern wall. He flinched, but now that he knew what it was, a new sensation flowed into his consciousness. He felt another presence, another force that was in his body and permeated the room at the same time.

"So," he said. "You work for Satan?"

"We prefer to call him Abaddon."

"So how does Mohammad Goldman, who I call the Raptor, fit into all this?"

"He is the Mahdi, the deliverer," he said. "We both work for the same master."

Another explosion prompted Diamond to pull out his phone again. "How far along are they? Okay good. You can now start disseminating the message that the Al Qaeda terrorist I am with is demanding one hundred million American dollars as retribution payment for the assassination of bin Laden, and safe passage for him and his accomplice in return for diffusing the nuclear weapon."

Django stared at Bernal who nodded.

Diamond stood with the briefcase in his hand. A brass ring on a string that went into the briefcase was attached to his right index finger. "Oh, and tell them the explosions are to open a passageway to get to the terrorists; that Al Qaeda has booby trapped the entire old city, and, uh, that all the other gates are rigged with nuclear weapons and they have sharpshooters all along the wall."

"None of that is true, is it?" Django asked.

"Partially true," he said. "We invented Al Qaeda, and then as these things usually go, it took on a life of it's own. We instigated the rebellions in North Africa, and look what happened. Anything is possible."

"What makes you think people will buy into any of this?"

He shrugged. "Fear, and experience. In times of hysteria, people will believe nearly anything. We've been spreading misinformation ever since the advent of mass communication. It's even easier now."

"So how are you going to hold off all the troops, the Iranians from blocking the Straits of Hormuz, the Israelis from attacking preemptively with their own nuclear weapons, the Chinese and Arabs from overrunning Jerusalem?"

Diamond pursed his lips. "We have them all in

abeyance at the moment because all eyes will soon be focused right here to see what happens?"

"Yeah, well, what about afterwards? What about if that bomb goes off anyway."

He shrugged. "It doesn't really matter. Abaddon's wishes will be fulfilled regardless. I'll either rule from behind the scenes here or in the next world as a deity. Besides, we control all the weapons systems and the computers that run them."

Another explosion echoed through Django's brain. The resultant crash of stones sounded as if they were getting closer to blasting through the wall.

"Shit," he exclaimed. "What if these explosions bring this dome down?"

"No problem." Diamond shrugged with his palms of his hands held upwards. "We'll be protected down here. Actually, it's part of our plan. It'll have to come down anyway, along with the Al Aqsa Mosque. The Jews will be allowed to build their third temple on this site after it's all over. Our seismologists figure that since this whole plateau is on landfill over an active fault line that they will probably come down on their own."

"Oh my God."

"Exactly."

Django gritted his teeth. "Does that mean the Jews

work for you?"

"Not directly," he said. "But as soon as any of these religions get organized after their prophet or avatar leaves the scene, we take over. Since the Jews were the first on the scene, we've just had a longer relationship with them."

"What about the Law of Moses, the Bible, the Quran?"

"None of this has been easy," he said. "Those were all good laws to live by, maybe even holy as they all claim, but in the end Abaddon always wins. Jesus was a tough one. What the bible doesn't tell you is that when Abaddon tempted him right on this mount to share dominion over this world, he accepted the modified plan. You notice that Christianity is the number one religion in the world."

"I don't buy that," he said.

"It doesn't matter."

Diamond answered his phone. "Okay, good."

"What now?" Django asked.

"Many countries are pledging millions to give to you terrorists. Seems like people will pay just about anything for peace." He smiled. "We'll probably take the money, but it doesn't really matter, we control all the central banks anyway. If we need currency, we just print some."

Another explosion. The cavern shook. Dust from the dome sparkled in the shaft of moonlight.

"What are you going to do with us?"

"Not sure," he said. "Maybe execute you as you try to make a getaway. I could let you talk to the press, but the world already thinks you're insane."

Django's cell vibrated.

"Can I answer this? Even condemned inmates get to make a call."

"Be my guest." He cackled.

"Can I have a moment of privacy? It's my girlfriend," he said. "I've heard that even the devil himself can be a gentleman."

Diamond shrugged and walked up the steps leading out of the chamber. "I'll give you thirty seconds," he said over his shoulder.

"Yeah?" Django whispered into the phone.

"I think the Raptor is headed up the Mount of Olives on horseback," Ghost answered. "What do you think?"

"Jump him and get the real spear to me. I need it for a bargaining chip."

"I don't know how, but I'll get it done."

A blast roared into both of his ears.

"Better make it fast," Django said.

Chapter 32
The Mahdi Rides

Ghost folded the sat phone and put it back in his pants pocket and turned to Celeste. Another blast from the Eastern Wall boomed through the Kidron Valley. They both recoiled.

"Django needs the spear in the Well of Souls." He stood and pointed. "And here comes the Raptor."

The Raptor's white robe and his ivory stallion gleamed in the moonlight. Even with the ambient light from the church, his regal image still shimmered.

Celeste rubbed her eyes. "What are we going to do?"

"Are you afraid of horses?" he asked.

"Maybe respectful is a better word," she said. "I ride in the Berkeley hills."

"I want you to distract him."

"You mean get in front of his horse?"

"If that's what it takes."

The edges of her mouth turned down. "I can't do that. I've also got this baby to protect."

He shook his head. "And after a one night mistake, you think it could be mine?"

"It's possible," she said. "The timing is right on the money."

"We have to make it out of here alive first," he said. "Here he comes."

"Okay, o-okay." She stammered. "I can't get in front of that huge horse. What do you want me to do?"

"It looks like the horse is just walking up the hill. Can you walk beside the horse when he gets close?"

"Maybe."

An explosion rocked the valley.

"You've got to try," he said.

"What are you going to do?"

Ghost stared down the hill. "Jump him and grab the spear. Just get his attention."

They both squatted in the moonlight. When he determined the Raptor's path, he motioned to Celeste. "Lay down behind that rock," he whispered. "When you see my signal, jump out."

"I don't like this," she whispered back.

When the horse's hooves were a dozen feet away, Ghost signaled for Celeste to jump out. When she did the horse reared and threw the Raptor to the ground. Ghost grabbed at the Raptor's white robe and it came completely off his body.

They rolled between the graves. Ghost felt that he could gain the advantage on his shorter adversary.

"Grab the reins," he yelled to Celeste.

The Raptor grabbed the spear that had fallen from his hands and lunged at Ghost. Another deafening explosion. Ghost dodged to his right, then came up and connected his right fist to the Raptor's chin. He rolled to the ground and Ghost hit him again knocking him out.

Below them, in the crease of the valley, the guards began running up the hill.

Ghost grabbed the spear out of the Raptor's hand and locked eyes with Celeste. "Do we run or fight?"

"Put on the Raptor's tunic and get on the horse," she yelled. "Head for the opening in the wall."

Ghost quickly donned the Raptor's white garment and jumped up onto his mount. "What about you?"

"They won't hurt me, especially if they know I'm pregnant," she said. "I'll tell them you kidnapped me."

"Great." He hugged her against his leg. Then, as he turned the horse downhill toward the pursuers, Celeste turned with him. "I'll find you," he said.

"I know you will. Keep your face shielded from them,

so they think you're him."

Ghost clenched his teeth and pulled the cap down to the top of his eyes and the gown up above his nose. "I love you."

"I love you, too."

The soldiers raised their guns. He noticed another person with them. *Lydia.* As he approached, he raised his hand and began to gallop. The soldiers shouldered their weapons.

"Father," Lydia yelled.

Ghost just waved and pointed toward the eastern wall.

When he reached the bottom of the Kidron Valley he looked up toward the Temple Mount. A rubble-strewn path had been blown open through the Golden Gate. The slope up to the gate was littered with rock and gravestones of the dead.

Tightening on the reins, he weaved his way through the chunks of debris. If they survived all this, what would he tell Django? What would he tell his wife for God's sake?

He passed through the Golden Gate, then stopped in front of the Dome of the Rock. In spite of the shelling of the western wall, no Israeli guards were stationed on the Temple Mount. They must be thick around the rest of the walls. He wondered how Diamond had held them off.

He pulled his phone out. "Anahita, are you still out

there?"

"Yes, I am," Her voice came back quickly.

"Where are you?" he asked.

"I'm by the Western Wall. Where are you?"

"I rode the Raptor's horse through the hole in the eastern wall," he said. "I've got the spear and I'm going to deliver it to Django. What's going on out there?"

"All hell is about to break loose," she said. "Everyone is waiting to see what happens with the negotiations."

"You mean peace negotiations at the U.N.?"

"No," she said. "You don't know, do you?"

"Know what?"

"That there's a nuclear weapon down there and Diamond is accusing Django of being an Al Qaeda terrorist," she said. "But the world knows the truth because there's a television reporter down there who has been broadcasting everything."

"Holy shit," he exclaimed. "Why don't you get the hell out of here?"

"I wanted to help, and like everyone else here, I want to be at the epicenter of history," she said. "And you my friend are at ground zero."

"This is unbelievable," he said. "I'm just a fisherman." He dismounted and walked toward the entrance to the Dome. An armed man wearing a black suit stood on the left side of the tiled archway, while an unarmed Waqf in Islamic garb stood on the right. The Muslin kneeled and bowed his head as he approached.

Ghost held up the spear. "I have the real thing."

The suit guy with the automatic weapon stayed rigid. He nodded quickly, then continued to swivel his head to survey the compound. "We've been expecting you."

Ghost pulled out his cell phone for a last communication with Anahita. "I'll have to get back to you. I'm going in."

"One other thing," she said. "Some people are saying you are Al-Mahdi, the Messiah."

"Oh Lord," he said to her as he entered the shrine.

Chapter 33
The Well of Souls

Inside the Well of Souls, Django paced. "You mean to tell me," he said to Diamond. "That you're going to try to convince the world that I'm a terrorist about to blow up the Dome of the Rock, Temple Mount and start World War III? Who's going to believe that?"

"Whomever I want to believe it."

"And what's my motive? Why would I want to do that?"

"You are demanding that Israel cede the West Bank, Gaza, Jerusalem and the Temple Mount to Palestine."

"That'll never happen."

Diamond flashed a demonic smile. "No, but it's a believable and doable demand."

Diamond's phone buzzed. "I told you not disturb me until I called."

He listened for a moment. "Yeah – yeah, okay."

Django and Bernal exchanged glances.

"Okay, I'll be looking for him," Diamond said to the caller.

Django squatted like a baseball catcher and ran his hands over the carpet on the floor of the cave. "Complications in your crazy scheme?"

"It seems your friend Ghost has a package for us," Diamond said.

Footsteps on the stairs echoed through the small chamber. They all turned as Ghost emerged. Candlelight danced against the walls of the well. Moonlight washed the steps behind him and beamed through the hole in the ceiling. His black face framed in the hood of the white robe was indeed a messianic vision to behold.

Diamond bowed. "Your highness."

"Don't give me that crap," Ghost said.

"Hey, buddy," Django said. "Will you give me the spear, please?"

Ghost handed it to him.

Django turned to Diamond. "This spear will make you the most powerful man in the world, giving you what you most desire. I'll hand it to you in exchange for that briefcase and free passage out of here for my friends and me."

Diamond scratched his chin. "What's to stop me from just taking it from you?"

Django looked around the room. "I'd say these three to one odds are stacked against you."

Diamond quickly pulled a .357 pistol out of the shoulder holster he wore. "Do you think I'd be crazy enough to come down here unarmed?" He snickered.

"I wouldn't put anything past you."

Diamond's phone buzzed. "Yeah, okay, send him in. Just make sure he's unarmed." He turned to Django. "We have another visitor – Mohammed."

Django exchanged glances with Ghost.

Soon the Raptor descended the stairs, saw Ghost, and then lunged for him. Django stood in his way and put his hands out to stop him.

"What's going on here?" the Raptor glared at Diamond.

"Seems we have a gathering of the tribes," Diamond said.

The Raptor pointed at Ghost. "Do you know that this man knocked me off al-Buraq, stole my robe, and is now threatening to ruin our plans. You have to kill these people. They know too much."

Django stepped toward the Raptor, but Diamond waved the gun at him.

"Stand down," Diamond ordered. "I'm in control here, and you will all do as I say."

"You better do something pretty quick," Django said.

"The whole world is holding its breath."

The air seemed to tighten as candlelight flickered against the walls. If he could distract Diamond for a moment, perhaps he could grab the .357 and the briefcase. The downside was unthinkable.

Diamond looked at each face. Django hoped he wouldn't find out that Bernal was recording the whole thing.

"The way I see it," Diamond said. "The world doesn't know who the Messiah is. All they know is that he is one of you, and that I am negotiating with the terrorists for the nuclear weapon in this briefcase." He lifted the satchel that held the bomb. The string was still firmly attached to his finger.

The Raptor's face was red. "We had a deal," he said. "You can't do this without me."

"Oh yes I can," Diamond said. "If someone else would make a better savior, so be it. It's better to be the kingmaker than the king."

Django gave a nearly imperceptible nod to Bernal who nodded back. The watch faced Diamond and the Raptor who stood next to him. "Well, I've got the spear, and I know how to wield the power," said Django. "Making the fate of the world resting with me."

"Will you swear allegiance to Abaddon and me?"

"Will you give me power and wealth?"

"It goes with dominion over the earth," Diamond said.

"Then we have a deal." Django reached out to shake his hand. As he did, the Raptor sprang for the gun. Diamond turned abruptly and shot the Raptor in the chest.

Django and Ghost moved in unison to jump on Diamond.

As Django grabbed the briefcase, Diamond pulled the string.

Chapter 34

Celeste and Lydia Act

The deafening explosion rocked the US Consulate that was less than ten minutes from the Temple Mount. Celeste locked eyes with Lydia. Would they be leveled by the ensuing nuclear wind? Was this it? Was this the end they feared, but had hoped would never happen?

"Turn on that TV," Celeste said to Lydia.

"What's the point?" she answered. "We're either dead or we're not."

"Okay, fine, I'll do it myself."

Celeste turned on the television in the small detention room of the American Consulate. They'd been taken there after the Israeli police in the Kidron Valley detained them. The Israeli's had their hands full and, although they were at first reluctant to turn them over to the Americans, they finally acquiesced to Celeste's demands. They really didn't have anything to hold them on anyway.

The television sprang to life. An announcer in front of the Western Wall quickly interrupted images of an American and Iranian naval battle in the Gulf of Hormuz. "There's been some kind of explosion from the top of the Mount," he said and pressed on his earpiece. "Just a second, just a moment. We're getting word that a Scud Missile has struck in the vicinity of the Al Aqsa Mosque. We don't yet have any reports of damage or casualties. As soon as we get any information, I will be back on the air."

Celeste was relieved. "Well at least it wasn't the nuclear device the terrorists have under the Dome of the Rock."

"How did you know about that?" she asked.

Celeste scanned the channels with the remote. "Bad news travels fast, plus I'm not as out of it as you think I am."

"The jury's still out on that," she said. "Keep searching the channels. I heard in the corridor that there was something going on at the Dome of the Rock."

Celeste stopped on Channel 10. "Here it is."

The station was running the last seconds of the shooting of the Raptor, followed by the struggle between Django and Diamond before the screen went blank. "And we don't know what happened after the fight," the announcer said. "We presume the nuclear weapon has not detonated. Back in a moment."

Lydia shrieked. "That's my father they shot."

"And that was Django grabbing for the suitcase."

"We have to get in there," Lydia said.

Celeste paced. "Well, they sort of have us detained here," she said. "We can't just walk over to the Temple Mount and demand that they let us in."

"We can try." Lydia stared at her. "That's my father who got shot and your boyfriend is fighting with a guy who has his hand on an atomic weapon."

"So, have you got any great ideas? I'm fresh out."

Lydia stared at the TV screen. "What about your Islamic friend? Maybe she can get us in."

"Anahita?" She barely knew her. "How could she help?"

"Well, she's Islamic, maybe she has some connections."

"She's also Iranian. I doubt that she has any pull in Jerusalem."

On the television, the Security Council was meeting at the United Nations. China had just vetoed a resolution to stop all hostilities in and around Israel, clinging to the notion that until Israel ceded the West Bank, Gaza, and old Jerusalem to the Palestinians, there could be no peace. Israel and her western allies were still adamant that all of

Jerusalem belonged to Israel.

"The world's people are holding their breath," said the announcer. "Until the situation under the Dome of the Rock is clarified. Meanwhile, we are starting to get video again from the Well of Souls."

Although the picture was grainy in the low light, Celeste could make out some faces. It looked like Django had a man in a headlock and Ghost held a gun.

"This is Lev Bernal," the announcer said. "We have just witnessed an extraordinary event here. Django Roth from the United States and a man who only gives his name as Ghost have just subdued a man they call Mr. Diamond, who claimed to have a nuclear weapon in his briefcase. This man, Diamond just shot well-known arms dealer, Mohammad Goldman. The situation seems stable at the moment, but we need medical assistance and security down here now."

Celeste glanced at Lydia. "Let's go."

"How?"

"They won't let us out of here on purpose," she said. "We could steal a consulate car, but we don't know where they keys are. Or, we could break out of here and run."

Lydia's eyes widened. "Run? What kind of shape are you in? "

"I can keep up with you." At least she hoped she could

keep up with Lydia's lean and mean body, but now wasn't
the time to show any weakness.

"Then let's go, sister."

There had been an American Marine outside their door,
but he was gone at the moment. They crept into the hallway
and headed for the back entrance. Once outside, they began
to run south. There were a few people milling in the streets,
but most were in their homes, either sleeping, watching the
news or praying that they would be alive in the morning to
see a new day.

After running for about five minutes Celeste stopped.
Her lungs ached and her legs felt leaden.

"What's the matter, sorority girl?"

"Okay, wise ass, I'm pooped. Let's see if we can find a
cab?"

Lydia's eyes narrowed. "At this hour? Why don't you
call your friend Anahita?"

"What can she do?"

"Well, for a couple of things," Lydia said. "She's
Muslim and can help us get onto the mount, and second, she
speaks all these languages."

"I guess you're right, this time." She pulled out her cell
phone and dialed Anahita.

At the intersection, a cab drove slowly west. Lydia
hailed it, and after no response, ran after the taxi.

A voice answered the call.

"Anahita, is that you?"

"Yes it is," she replied.

"Where are you?"

"I'm in front of the Mugrahbi Gate."

"Can you get us onto the Temple Mount and then into the Dome of the Rock?"

There was a pause and some muffled conversation. A cab stopped next to the curb. Lydia threw open the rear door, and Celeste climbed in with the phone still up to her ear.

"I might be able to get you in," Anahita finally answered. "But you better keep quiet when you get here. I'll have to do all the talking."

Celeste looked at Lydia who stared out the window. "I'll do the best I can to try to keep her quiet."

Lydia's head spun around. "Listen bitch." She gritted her teeth. "You don't control me, but we both know we better cooperate if we want everyone to come out of this in one piece."

They quickly arrived at the walls of the old city where they simultaneously jumped out of opposite sides of the taxi.

"Pay the man," Celeste said.

Lydia rummaged through her pants pockets. "All I have

is a few Belizean dollars and plastic."

"Perfect," she said. "How is it all you rich people never pay for anything?"

Celeste pulled a twenty dollar bill out and handed it to the driver, expecting that he would give her change."

"No American," he said. "Only shekels. No change."

"You're a crook," she said. "Take this or nothing."

The driver grabbed the bill, jumped back in the driver's seat and sped off.

Celeste burned as she watched him disappear down a side street. "We support this country no matter what they do and this is what I get?" She flipped him the bird.

Lydia grabbed her arm and they waded into the crowd, pushing their way forward until they got to the entrance. Anahita stood with an Israeli soldier and a Waqf guard. She spoke to each of the men and they let all three of the women into the compound.

"What did you say to them?" Celeste asked.

The slightest smile crossed Anahita's face. "Let's just say that if we live through this, I'll have a couple of engagements I'll need to honor."

The three women walked to the center of the Temple Mount. The Dome gleamed in the moonlight. Some soldiers gathered around the Scud crater near Al-Aqsa Mosque.

"Well, here we go," Lydia said.

Celeste took the lead as they walked toward the center of the world's attention. She knew that whatever happened in the next few minutes would change her life forever.

Chapter 35

The Confession

Django had Diamond in a headlock with his left arm and a hammerlock with his right arm when security entered the cavern and took the director into custody. Medics were attending to the Raptor who had sustained a wound in his lower left shoulder above his heart. Bernal continued to broadcast the story on Channel 10.

Django turned his head toward the stairs as the sound of footsteps caught his attention. The guards drew their weapons.

He recognized Celeste first. "Put your guns down," he said. "These women belong here."

The Captain of the Guard was reluctant to shoulder his automatic. "Who are these women, and why are they here?"

"The taller brunette is Celeste, my fiancée; the shorter woman in black is Lydia, Mohammad's daughter; and the Muslim woman is my friend Anahita, who saved my life."

The captain turned to one of the guards. "Search them."

"Face the wall, put your hands against it and spread your legs," the guard ordered.

When he had searched them thoroughly he turned back to the captain. "They're clean, sir."

Celeste walked over to Django and hugged him, then she turned to Ghost and did the same with him.

"How did you get in here?" Django asked Celeste

"Anahita worked some magic," she said.

Django felt Celeste's stomach. "How are you feeling?"

"Not bad considering."

Django watched Lydia who tried to comfort her father who writhed in pain.

"I guess it could be worse," he said.

"I've heard that half the world thinks you guys are some kind of saviors," she said. "Our lives are going to be quite different when we get out of here."

"A quiet life in Berkeley sounds pretty good for awhile."

She looked at the floor. "I don't know about that."

"Oh really?" This was something he hadn't considered. "Do you have other plans?"

Celeste pointed to Lydia. "She's offered me a job in Belize as her head artist for a lot more money than I could ever make teaching at Cal."

Bernal pointed his watch camera at Django. "Please put that down," Django said. "Haven't you got everything you need? This is extremely personal."

Bernal nodded and moved to interview the captain.

Django turned to Celeste. "What about the house and the baby?"

"I can't live like this," she said. "I will always love you, but you will never change. You'll always be a professional drifter."

Django stared up at the shaft of moonlight that shone through the hole in the cavern. She was right about his insatiable urge to keep moving, but, in this case, he wanted her love as much as he wanted the money for the spear to get the care for his father, and fund the next hunt.

"How long will you stay?" he asked.

"I'm not sure," she said. "They have their own highly rated medical staff on the island."

"What about all your stuff at the house?"

"You can send me what I need. It won't be much."

Ghost, who had been observing the conversation, hugged Celeste.

Django stared at both of them. "I guess everybody got what they wanted."

"Well," Ghost said. "You got the spear back and according to the word on the street, World War III has been temporarily averted as the UN sorts all these issues out."

"Yeah, I've got the spear, but I never got anything for it to help my dad." He looked around the room. "Just a lot of grief."

The medics had stabilized the Raptor and now carried him up the steps. Lydia followed and as she passed, grabbed Celeste by the arm. "Are you coming?"

"Yes," Celeste said. "But first, we've got some business to attend to with rather limited funds."

Lydia searched their eyes, then approached Django. "What if I give you a million dollars for the spear?"

Both spears lay on the carpeted floor of the cavern. The real one was the closest to them.

"Which one?" he asked.

Lydia looked at each of the spears. "Are you a gambling man?"

"Usually I am," he said.

"Then let's have a neutral person, say like Anahita hold the two spears behind her back and one of us picks an arm."

He knew there wasn't any way to rig the results. Was he willing to take the chance of selling off the real spear for a mere million? Did he want the burden of the legitimate artifact anyway? The million dollars would go a long way to helping his dad.

"Let's do it," he said.

Anahita picked up the two spears. She put the real one in her right hand and the counterfeit in her left hand, and then backed away from them toward the wall.

The guards led a handcuffed Diamond up the stairs. The captain lingered as Bernal continued to film.

"Who picks?" Django asked. He didn't know if Anahita knew which was the real one, and even if she did, she might switch them behind her back. For some reason, he thought of football, and how the team that won the toss in overtime always wanted to go on defense first so they would know exactly what they had to do.

"You want to flip a coin?" Lydia rummaged through her pockets.

"No," he said. "Ladies first."

"So after all this insanity, you remain a gentleman."

He shrugged. He was either going to get a lot of money for a fake spear, or Lydia would soon become the richest and most powerful woman in the world. In spite of the consequences, he would have his money. He'd take those odds.

"I'll take the sword in her right hand," she said.

Anahita handed her that spear. Lydia took it and examined the blade. "I think I made a pretty good choice."

"I think so too." He took the other spear from Anahita.

Celeste kissed Django and headed up the stairs with

Lydia. She turned. "Will I see you soon?"

"I imagine so," he said. "We don't have any way back to Belize except in Lydia's Learjet. Plus I have to make sure I get the money."

Lydia laughed. "I'm good for it."

"I'll make sure of that," Celeste said.

He walked toward the stairs. "And how about that ride for me and Ghost?"

"You got it, cowboy," Lydia said. "I have to check to see what they're going to do with my father, and then get the plane ready to go. We'll meet you at the Atarot airport around daybreak."

Celeste shot him a thin smile and they disappeared into the moon glow in the dome.

"So," Ghost said. "Which one did you get?"

"I don't know yet." He turned the blade over in his hand. "They are exact duplicates. I can't tell until I dig into the handle, but I think she got the real one."

"I don't think so," Anahita said.

"How would you know?"

"I could feel the energy of the real spear pulsing up my arm," she said. "The real one was in my right hand. When she picked that arm, I switched them behind my back."

"Why would you do that?" he asked.

"I'd rather you have the real spear than her. This world

has seen too much violence and I know you're basically a kind and gentle man."

He hugged her.

The captain of the guard walked up to them. He'd been talking on his cell phone. "I understand you're seeking asylum in the United States," he said to Anahita.

"Yes I am," she said.

"It's been granted."

"How did that happen so fast?"

"Our country, the US and you have a friend in common." He stared into her eyes.

"Who?"

The captain handed her the phone.

"Hello, who is this?" she asked.

Django watched the tears well in her eyes.

"Mehdi!" she exclaimed.

"I'll leave you gentlemen down here for a few minutes," the captain said to Django, Ghost and Bernal. "While I escort this new American to the airport. She might be going home with you."

Bernal turned his watch camera toward Ghost and Django who stood together in the center of the room. "By now we must have millions of viewers from around the world watching this global, yet very personal drama play out. Do either of you have any final words to add to this incredible story?"

Django looked at Ghost, dressed as the conquering Messiah, while he himself was dressed as an Islamic worshipper. A non-practicing, drifting Jew and a Rastafarian fisherman were supposed to say something profound to a spiritually hungry world.

He deferred to Ghost with a gesture of his open palms.

"I don't really know what to say," Ghost said. "I didn't really want to be here. I came to help my friend and we got caught up in this whirlwind of politics."

"So is either of you the promised Moshiach?"

"No, I am not," Ghost replied quickly.

Bernal turned to Django. "Are you?"

Django looked into the eye of the camera. "I am no more the anointed one than any of the people out there watching this. We are all a part of God and we are all one. Find the peace and love within yourself and share it with your family and friends. Look for your savior within."

His short talk left Bernal and Ghost temporarily speechless.

Finally Bernal pointed the watch at himself. "Well, you've heard it all. It remains to be seen what will happen to Israel, but we have witnessed a remarkable event. As this day progresses into morning, we'll see if any of this has made a difference to the politicians eager for war. We'll see if Jew, Muslim and Christian can indeed live in peace, especially on this most holy of mountains in the most holy of cities. This is Lev Bernal signing off for now from the Well of Souls. Hope to see you tomorrow."

Chapter 36

Farewell

The flight back to the Raptor's island had been quiet. Except for a refueling stop, it had been an uneventful trip. Django knew that everyone was emotionally spent. He traded off with Ghost assisting Lydia at the controls and keeping her awake with small talk. With Anahita opting to fly to the US on a commercial flight out of Tel Aviv, and he and Ghost quietly in deep thought, Celeste had no one to talk to, so she slept nearly the entire trip.

"The island looks smaller," he said to Lydia.

Lydia stared at her instrument panel, turning switches in her approach. "They say everything looks smaller after you grow up."

"It's only been a few days."

"And a lifetime of changes," she said.

"Perhaps so," he said. "How are you going to pay me for the spear?"

"How do you want it?"

"Do you have cash?"

Lydia keyed her headset. "Roger that. Cleared to land. Thank you." She turned her head toward him. "I might be able to rustle it up. You're awfully brazen."

"Well," he said. "You do have possession of perhaps the most valuable spiritual relic in the world. I believe I have the right to expect maximum security in this transaction."

The runway appeared in front of them. "Will you take Belizean dollars?"

"Two million of them," he said.

"I thought we were talking one million Belizean."

"Please, we know what the agreement entailed, and what kind of currency we were talking. No games, okay."

The jet bounced on the runway, came to a quick stop, and then taxied to the main elevator. Lydia departed first, then Ghost, then Django helped Celeste down the steps.

A group of guards met them on the tarmac, but Lydia walked over and talked to them. Then they left.

The group descended in the elevator and walked to Lydia's office.

"Lock the door," she said.

Ghost locked the door, and then stood guard. Django and Celeste sat in the two chairs in front of her large desk, as Lydia dialed the combination to a floor safe.

She pulled out a strong box and laid it on the desktop, and counted out two hundred ten thousand dollar bills. "Are you satisfied?" she asked.

Django held one up to the light. "Are they good?" he asked.

Lydia narrowed her eyes. "We do run the Central Bank."

"Fair enough." He stuffed the bills into his leather duffel bag on top of the real spear. "Now, I assume you'll guarantee our safe passage off the island?"

"For you and Ghost?"

"Yes," he said. "I also assume that Celeste is still staying here with you."

They both looked at Celeste who lowered her gaze and then nodded.

"Then, I guess we're done here," he said.

He certainly didn't want it to end this way. The walk to the dock felt in some ways like the final march of a dead man walking to his execution. He was about to leave behind the woman with whom he had lived for nearly twenty years. It just didn't feel right.

Rain barked as they approached. He was one happy dog, and had obviously been well taken care of during their time in the Middle East.

Ghost grabbed his dog by the neck and let him lick wildly at his face. Then Django wrestled Rain to the ground and rolled around with him until they both had enough.

Django got to his feet and dusted himself off. "Okay, let's get out of here."

Ghost jumped on the boat and fired up the engine. She started right up. Django shook hands with Lydia, and then put his arms around Celeste's neck.

He stared deeply into her eyes. "I hope this is a passing phase."

"I don't think so," she said. "But I appreciate the concern."

He kissed her on the lips. "This is hard. I really don't want to leave you."

Tears ran down her cheeks. "I know."

Rain jumped onboard, and Django untied the line from the stern, then moved to the bow and untied the rope from the cleat. He pushed the boat away from the dock, and then jumped over the rail.

Lydia put her arm around Celeste, and they waved together as Ghost backed the craft slowly away.

As Rain barked, Django waved. A major part of his life faded into the afternoon sun.

He and Ghost hadn't spoken since they pushed away

from the dock. The mesmerizing rhythm was hypnotic to sailors. Django needed the sensory deprivation anyway.

Finally Ghost broke the silence. "Well, what do you think, bud? That was quite a trip."

"I don't know, man," he said. "It's a load. I lost my lover. My best friend betrayed me. I nearly got killed. I was at the epicenter of a possible world war."

"And you still have the spear, and you're a millionaire."

"Yeah, there is that."

"And you'll be able to get the care for your father that he needs."

"That's true," he said. "And what about you?"

"What about me?"

"Are you going to tell your wife that you may have gotten Celeste pregnant?"

"There's no need to do that," he replied. "We don't know that yet."

"We will before the year is over."

"Then I will deal with it then."

Ghost's Cay was now in sight. Rain stood on the bow and barked. Django rubbed his neck.

"When did you make love with Celeste, man?" Django asked.

"I didn't tell you that I came to Berkeley looking for you and you were gone, as usual. Celeste was lonely and I was weak. It only happened once."

"Yeah, and how did you think I was going to take this?"

Ghost gazed across the water and steered into the wind. "Honestly, I didn't think about you. I gave into lust."

"That's a killer, man." He checked the dock lines. "How do you expect me to trust you again?"

"I guess I'm going to have to earn it back somehow."

Ghost eased the boat up to his dock. Django jumped out and pulled it up to the back of his own sailboat that was still tied to the dock.

"You're supposed to be this meditative, spiritual guy," Django said to Ghost who stacked gear on the dock. "How do you resolve this with your religion?"

Ghost jumped out of the boat. "I don't little brother. I can't. I'm a sinner like everyone else in our flawed species. But, I believe in redemption."

"Redemption?" Django threw his pack into the back of his boat and set the duffel bag next to his guitar case. "What redemption is there in betraying a friend?"

"God's redemption is infinite," he said. "I just pray for forgiveness, practice forgiveness and try to cultivate my own loving responses to adversity. That's all I can do."

"I'll try to do the same," he said. "But none of this is going to be easy."

"Nobody said it was an easy path."

Django jumped over the gunnel wall. "I didn't expect it to be easy."

"Do you want your carbon dating instruments in the shanty?"

He looked toward the shack. The waves lapped up against the conch shells. "I don't think so, man. I think they're pretty messed up anyway. You can have 'em. I think I can afford some new equipment now anyway." He smiled.

Ghost untied his lines. "When am I going to see you again?

"When we all heal," he said. "You owe me a visit to California."

They hugged, and Ghost pushed him away. Rain jumped into the water and swam after his boat,

"Rain, go back," Django yelled.

Rain kept swimming. Ghost just stood and watched.

"Call for him," Django yelled to Ghost.

"I think he's made his choice," Ghost yelled back.

When Rain got near the boat, Django reached over and pulled him aboard.

"I'll bring him right back," he yelled.

"He's yours little brother. My gift."

After Rain shook the water off his coat, Django rubbed his head. He knew the significance of Ghost's gesture. Some things were more precious than possessions.

He waved to his friend, now bathed in the golden wash of the Caribbean sunset.

Epilogue

He'd been drifting and sailing all night on calm seas, and now the sun was rising on a new day. Rain sat at the bow staring into the red and golden Caribbean sunrise. The spear lay on top of his backpack next to his guitar.

"What do you think, boy?" He looked at Rain who happily wagged his tail in response. "That was a hell of a trip."

He calibrated the GPS and set the boat to auto-pilot, then picked up his guitar and began to sing Leonard Cohen's Hallelujah: "And even though it all went wrong, I'll stand before the Lord of Song with nothing on my tongue but Hallelujah. Hallelujah, Hallelujah, Hallelujah, Hallelujah."

Then, he put down the guitar, picked up the spear and held it against the rising sun. What was he going to do with it now? What if the legends were true and he was now the most powerful man in the world. How crazy was that?

Rain ambled from the front of the boat and perched like a lion in front of him. "Are you cool with all this?" he asked his new companion.

The Golden Lab just licked the air. Maybe he smiled.

Django thought about Celeste going off with Lydia. He'd have to adjust to a new life without her. Maybe she left because she'd been mostly without him for the last twenty years. What if he was the father of her baby now gestating in her stomach? Would he be willing to give up the life of a professional drifter to settle down as a father? Celeste had behaved like she knew the answer to that before he did.

A squall gathered to the west, so he took the helm again. Rain followed him to the back of the boat. The first puff of wind hit him in the face. He adjusted his tack to beat into the wind.

Maybe he should throw the spear into the ocean and rid the world of one artifact that fueled the insatiable quest for power. Let it sink to the bottom of the sea where no man or woman would ever be tempted again to try to dominate the world. Perhaps ending one of the chief symbols of world power would be a disincentive for any future would-be conqueror.

He knew better. As Ghost always said, "If you took all the money and power in the world and redistributed it equally to the citizens of the earth, in six months it would be back in the same hands."

He pulled a book out of his pack and read a quote from the great sage Lao Tzu: "Be content with what you have; rejoice in the way things are. When you realize there is nothing lacking, the whole world belongs to you."

Ghost came to the forefront of his thoughts. He may never understand how his friend betrayed him. Perhaps some day he would, but that time wasn't now.

Now was the time to sail to Miami, turn in the boat and fly back to Berkeley to pick up the pieces of his life. He needed to visit his dad in that run-down nursing home and get him the care he needed. That's why he put his life at risk. He'd do again in a green flash.

The surging waves tossed the boat like a toy. Rain hunkered down near the mast. He slipped on his slicker, grabbed the spear and tucked it into his pack just before a rogue wave hurled the boat sideways tossing everything to the starboard side.

"Hang on, boy," he yelled.

The pack and the spear flew by Rain and headed for the drink. Django abandoned the tiller and lunged for the pack and spear just as they were about to go overboard. The boat and mainsail tossed and swung as if Providence played with a trinket.

He grabbed the spear, slung it back in the pack, and then grabbed Rain and pulled him under his feet. After the deck looked secure, he grasped the tiller.

The squall was losing steam. Within minutes the skies began to clear and the sun peaked through.

Isn't this the way it goes? Isn't this the way the universe tries to teach me now, or the lesson comes around again and again and again until I get it right?

The only thing he knew for sure was that The Spear of Christ wasn't done with him yet.

CPSIA information can be obtained at www.ICGtesting.com
Printed in the USA
LVOW071735260911

247936LV00002B/101/P